Gilligan's Last Elephant

Gilligan's

CLEVELAND AND NEW YORK

GERALD HANLEY

Last Elephant

THE WORLD PUBLISHING COMPANY

PUBLISHED BY *The World Publishing Company*

2231 WEST 110TH STREET, CLEVELAND 2, OHIO

LIBRARY OF CONGRESS CATALOG CARD NUMBER: 62-15716

SECOND PRINTING

To 1463 Lance Corporal Ahamed Hussein of the Shekál, interpreter of many things, and to Hirad Barri and all the Midgan hunters, wherever they may be wandering

Contents

I. The Men

1

It was over twelve years since Gilligan had camped in this spot beside the Waso Larok River, and nothing had changed. The river still flowed wide and brown, like thin glistening oil in the glare of the sun. The huge mimosa thorns still threw the same broken lacework shadows on the red sand, and there was the same ancient silence. Nothing had changed. He braked the slowly rolling truck to a stop and stared through the dusty windshield at the far blue hills across the river. Up there in those hills was the elephant Muller wanted.

He got out of the truck and shouted for a bottle of beer. Aganaza, sitting on top of the truck with the gun-bearer, Jama, smiled through his mask of red dust and lifted a bottle of cold beer out of the water-filled canvas bucket he always had ready on safari. Gilligan took it from him, opened it with an opener he kept on a key chain, and then went and sat down under a thorn tree with it.

"*Fungua vyombo,*" he called to Aganaza. "We camp here." The cold beer hit his palate with an excruciating tingle. He drank half of it and wiped his mouth with the back of his big, hairy, sinewy hand. Then he lit a cigarette.

"Happy," he said, "happy," and leaned back against the tree and watched his Africans unload the big truck. Bwana first, as always. Camp table, canvas chairs, water bottles, rifles, hurricane lamps, the chop-box containing the canned food and booze, hurriedly and smoothly the two African servants set up Gilligan's area of the camp.

Did he want tea? No, another two cold beers. Tea in an hour. For dinner he would have the chops of the eland he had shot in the afternoon, and some of the liver. Aganaza listened and nodded and then went away to make his kitchen fire.

The tracker, Chongu, was waiting back at Guyu for Muller and would guide him down here tomorrow. Until then Gilligan could laze. "Happy," he said again, reaching for the beer.

He was fifty-seven and still did not fret about approaching age, still felt no twinges, still moved limberly and could shoot down a beast with the same speed and ease as when he had begun killing over thirty years before. A hater of civilization, he was short-tempered in places like Nairobi, Mombasa, Arusha, Dar es Salaam, or anywhere in which the ant-men had put up their huddles of cement buildings and cinemas and shops. The ant-men were all those who clung together among buildings and bought and sold things until they died and were put into a cemetery among the rows of other ant-men who had gone before them. The only Africans the ant-men ever met were their cooks, to whom few of them could talk anyway, but they were ready always to pronounce on the problems of Africa and the Africans. After two days in Nairobi he always got into a quarrel with some of the ant-men. He could not stand by in the bars and listen to their chatter about the things they knew nothing about. All the way down here he had mulled over the row he had had with two of them in the New Stanley Bar. Two new ones they were, clerk types, and he had given them both hell after overhearing their maddening views on the future of Africa. They had heatedly argued back and he had offered to fight both of them. They had refused. Typical of the ant-men. Big talk and no action.

Now, though, drinking the cold beer in the enormous hot silence by the river, he savored the pleasure of being alone, and unreachable by anyone except Chongu and Muller. No one else knew where he was. No one could pester him or annoy him with their half-baked opinions about everything from the Bomb to the color problem. He opened another beer.

This American, Muller, must not only be rich, but eccentric as well. "Expense is no object," he had written. "I just want the best elephant left in the country. You can write your own check." So he was going to give him the bull which had nearly killed him twelve years ago, but which had killed a fellow called Pratt instead and had then got away in the fast-falling darkness. That bull had frightened him, the only beast ever to achieve that. He could still see its huge old-fashioned tusks, of a size which had vanished after the coming of smokeless powder and the truck. He always thought of that bull as his own. It lived in country so hard and cruel that no one ever went there. There was a hell of scrub and rock to cross before that country was reached, as he had written and warned Muller, who had been offended and had written back to say that he liked it tough. "The tougher the better for me. Nothing can shake me. I like it tough." Gilligan had felt a resentment after reading those lines in Muller's letter. He did not like people to assume themselves to be tough, for he had never met anyone as tough as himself.

'We'll see, mister,' he thought somberly while drinking the beer. 'We'll see. You like it tough? Right. You'll get more than you want.' All the American's letters rang with that kind of vanity, a sort of exhibitionistic enthusiasm about the tough life. "I hate the goddam city. Give me the wilderness anytime. Were you in the war?"

'Was *I* in the war?' Gilligan fumed when he thought of it. He had been in both the wars and had enjoyed them both, wished they could be fought again. There ought to be a war going on somewhere all the time, a war to which people like himself could go. In a sane world Australia or some other huge waste would have been put aside as a permanent battleground for men to fight on. These were thoughts which he had learned never to express to people. They simply did not understand what he was talking about.

"Tough, are you?" he said aloud, thinking of Muller's last letter. "We'll see."

He got up and stretched, a big, heavy-shouldered man in his khaki shorts and bush shirt. He never wore stockings and his long legs were dark reddish brown from constant sunburn. The heavy Somali sandals sewn with white camel sinew suited him, went well with his wild shock of graying yellow hair. Like all men who have lived alone in wilderness for years, he carried on long conversations with himself, aloud. Even though he tried to remember not to do it, regarding it as a very bad sign in a white man, he talked to himself most of the time. His African nickname was *Bwana Peki Yaki*, meaning the "lonely one," though to Gilligan himself it signified "the one who is out on his own," "the one who is special, unique," for he knew he was unique, and he never felt lonely.

He finished the beer and then sent for his new gun-bearer, Jama, a man whom he was trying to like, for Jama was a Somali and Gilligan had never been able to like Somalis. They had nearly killed him once, the Somalis; up beyond Mandera it was, about fifteen years ago, after he had struck one of them, one who had argued heatedly with him, a thing so shocking that he had not been able to put up with it. The rest of the Somali *kariya* had come to his camp that night for revenge, and he had had to get out of it after wounding two of them with rifle fire. He had had several brushes with Somalis since, gladly, for their arrogance, their refusal to be awed or properly respectful, their excitability in argument, always fired his temper. They did not behave like Africans, but were proud, handsome, obsessed by their feeling of nobility, could not be bullied or cowed, loved quarrel and litigation, and cherished a wrong until it was paid for.

He had not wanted to take on Jama after the death of his old gunbearer, but Jama's record was excellent, and in a fine mood of "Can't condemn the whole race after all," Gilligan had decided he would try Jama. One thing you could always know about any Somali, even if you had never met him, was that he had guts, and Jama seemed a pleasant enough personality.

He came striding up at Gilligan's call, a tallish, slender, fit man of about forty with narrow, handsome, black features. His nose was finely nostriled, a straight perfect ancient Egyptian nose, and his large black eyes were shrewd and calm. He was wearing khaki shorts and a bush shirt, a brightly colored cotton skullcap, and a gold wrist watch. Gilligan had taken a dislike to the wrist watch. He never liked to see an African with a wrist watch, even though he knew it was unreasonable. It always angered him and made him suspicious, that kind of thing. He never liked to see an African using a fountain pen or glasses, horn-rimmed ones especially, and he would never allow an African to speak English to him. He did not know why it was, but there was always a suggestion of familiarity and intimacy in an African who spoke in English, as if some necessary mystery between him and the African were being dissolved. There were times when he knew he was too touchy and unreasonable about these things, and that he was "bush happy" and eccentric, but he could not help himself. "When you hate a black," he often told people, "get rid of him fast." And he liked Africans, knew the virtues of the various tribes, but he resented the drift toward change which he saw in them. It was only during the past few years that he had given up resenting their wearing of shorts and bush shirts. He liked them primitive and innocent and trusting, as if the virtue and courage would go out of them with the putting on of shorts and the taking up of fountain pens.

Before he knew he was doing it he said to Jama, "Where did you get that watch? It's gold, isn't it?" Jama had only been with him for three days, and they were studying each other all the time.

Jama looked at the watch on his wrist and then smiled at Gilligan, looking into his pale blue eyes to see what was there. He saw a faint cold hostility, but no more than usually appeared in this kind of blue eye in a white man; yet he was edgy when he replied.

"I bought it," he said. "Do you like it? It is a good watch. I bought it in Mogadishu last year."

"How much was it?"

"Three hundred shillings," said Jama.

"That's a lot of money." Gilligan watched Jama's steady eyes, looking for something, seeing only a calm, black, level stare.

"I've got plenty of money," Jama told him. "I don't need to work, but I like safari. I have tried to settle down with my wife and camels, but I get restless and have to go again." He laughed at his own waywardness, his splendid teeth shining with a film of spittle. "We are all the same, we hunters," he said. "We cannot settle. You too like the bush life. I cannot live in a town."

These were Gilligan's own sentiments, but Jama was too free and easy, and not since Gilligan had taken him on had Jama once called him Bwana, which was what this meeting was about.

"Now we're in the bush, Jama," Gilligan said, meeting his eyes with a look of quiet and confident command, "I'm boss. You call me Bwana. Understand? Bwana. And don't give any orders without consulting me. I heard you shouting at Aganaza. Stop it. That's my order. Call me Bwana, and give no orders unless I tell you to give them. That way we'll get on fine. Have you understood me?"

"*Ndio, Bwana,*" Jama said, smiling slowly, yet not impudently, but Gilligan watched the smile and felt around it, studying Jama's eyes for insolence, but could find none. But the smile was wrong, was Somali in its assumption, in its lack of a proper understanding of reproof. 'That'll do for now,' Gilligan thought. 'I'll take it nice and slow.' Because he suspected all Somalis, and had been made frightened by them that night north of Mandera years ago, and because of their reputation for *fitina*, trouble and quarrel, he was tempted to rush them, to overcome them, to crush them and make them like the other Africans, the Bantu. He knew this vaguely with half his mind and he told Jama he could go back to the campfire.

It was when Jama had gone that Gilligan felt one of his faint pangs of regret, almost remorse. He knew he was oversuspicious, too touchy and ready to find trouble where there was none, but as usual he dismissed the regret.

"You're bush happy, Gill," he told himself aloud, opening another bottle of beer. "The blacks are getting you down. Don't let them do it. Take things easy." But he was sorry he had taken on Jama and he missed his old gunbearer, who had been a friend. He was sorry he had taken on Jama because he knew that he was going to have trouble with him, and that he would make it himself.

2

JAMA WAS IN SUCH A TEMPER when he got back to the
campfire that he was trembling with it, having several
times gone over the scene he had just been through with
Gilligan, tasting the insults and insinuations in Gilligan's
eyes and voice, especially about the watch. It was obvious now that Gilligan resented his having a *gold* watch,
for he had used the word for gold, *dhahabu*, as if somebody like him, Jama, had no right to such precious stuff.
As vain as Gilligan, Jama had known from the start that
he was going into the employ of the kind of white man
who wanted anyone with a black skin to act like a mem-
ber of a lower order of the human race. He had worked
for such a white man before and had vowed never to
work for another, but there were good reasons why he
must go back on his vow just now. He would have to
put up with Gilligan's ways as best he could if ever he was
to get to America. It was because Gilligan was taking a

rich American on safari that Jama had offered his services. There had been many good omens in the business: being there in Guyu township and being told that Gilligan needed an experienced gunbearer, and then being told that Gilligan was taking an American to shoot elephant. There were good omens of all kinds in the business, for he had been about to apply for a job with the game department, been ready once again to shelve his dream of going to America to get an education. His country was soon going to be free and he saw himself as a leader, an ambassador, an important person one day if only he were sensible now. And he belonged to a noble, leading tribe. Was he too old, though? He had had some education in Abyssinia under the Italians, and had enjoyed it, and had enjoyed soldiering for them even more. He had risen to sergeant major during the war, proud of his intelligence and courage, and had fought through the battle with the British at Gar Buluk, where he had seen that some white men did not like to die as readily as Somalis. He was not impressed by white men as white men, though he had met many he had liked and respected, but as a race they possessed no mystique or magic for him.

He sat down by the fire and brooded, forcing his plans on himself, determined that all would come out as he dreamed it.

After a few minutes of his wild dreams and plans he became despondent, as usual, knowing it would all come to nothing and that it was too late for these plans. He had never been able to save money. He spent it as fast as he earned it, and he liked to throw a handful of coins to the beggars near a mosque. He was burdened with a wife and children, and he missed them only rarely. His life and experiences had taken him far beyond that narrow, sure routine of tribal life in the wilderness behind the camels, but he knew that he would end there, behind the camels, and that he would choose it. Like all Somalis, the greatest wanderers in Africa, he was ready to be a barman in New York and a half-naked spearman again afterwards.

"Come and help to unload the truck," Aganaza shouted. "This is no time to sit by the fire. Come and help us."

"You needn't shout about it," Jama yelled back, rising from his haunches. "You send the *toto* to call me if you want me. Don't shout at me." Angry again, he walked to the truck to have a few heated words with Aganaza, one of those subservient, brainless members of the slave races. He was sorry he had come on this safari now. He did not like any of the people he was with. What would the American be like?

3

GILLIGAN HAD BEEN WARNED TWICE by the game department during the last three years, about things they could not prove, but they knew he had been poaching. He had lost his license to take clients out some years before, not for poaching, but for what one client had called "unbearable and insulting behavior." This client had summed up what some others had spoken about in the bars after returning from safari with Gilligan, describing how Gilligan was pugnacious, even dangerous, quarrelsome, and altogether antisocial, and should not be allowed to have any dealings with clients.

The fact was that Gilligan felt he owned Africa, and resented any other white people being there. He was jealously possessive of the country and for years had been getting worse in his cantankerous moods. He had refused to let one client do any shooting at all and had called the whole safari off when hundreds of miles from

civilization, refusing to move until the client agreed to
return to Nairobi. In his defense, when questioned about
this, Gilligan had said, "I didn't like the fellow. He was
too bloody boastful, couldn't use a rifle anyway, and
got on my nerves with his ways in general. I wouldn't
put up with his continual arguing. These people shouldn't
be allowed into Africa at all. They're not wanted."

Any hint by a stranger that he knew something about
game or the bush always put Gilligan into a hostile frame
of mind. Only with one or two old-timers like himself
could he feel at ease, and he seldom came across old
acquaintances now, except for Graig.

"The thing is, Gill," one young game warden had said
to him during one of his troubles with the law, "the thing
is that you belong to another time altogether. Everything's changed. you can't just go and do what you like
nowadays. You behave as if Livingstone had just died.
And you'd better watch out. We know you've been
poaching. Put your gun away and get a job."

But he could not settle, could not work for anybody.
The only job he had held down for a time was a contract
for shooting rhinoceros out so as to make way for sisal
plantations in a remote piece of territory. He had done
well out of that job. "I was left alone, that's why," he
would explain. "If only they'd leave you alone, these
bloody people who know nothing about what's to be
done."

His life had been a series of disasters since leaving the
army after the First World War. As a soldier-settler he
had drawn a farm out of the hat, had grown maize, and
had seen it eaten twice by the locust swarms. He had had
no capital and had gradually sunk to eating *posho* like

an African or an old-time Dutchman, and had finally sold the land and then drunk the money. He vanished for some years toward Abyssinia, making the country between the Juba and the Tana rivers his enormus arid home.

He was physically very powerful and developed a mania for being more powerful than other people, and was, performing feats of strength in bars or sitting at tables in Indian wrestling bouts with men willing to take him on.

"It's all a matter of tension," he would say. "Not just muscle, but psychological. Take me, for instance. *I'm* perfectly made and my mind and body mesh, like the gears of a car. A combination like that is unbeatable. You're wasting your time. What'll you bet, five quid?" The annoying thing for those who knew him was that he was right. He had never found anyone as strong as himself, in Indian wrestling, bending pieces of iron, lifting heavy chairs by the base of one of the legs. And he was even vainer about his shooting, which was first class.

Those who knew him usually left a bar as soon as he came into it. He knew he was not popular and could not understand it. This knowledge had merely increased his pugnacity and his readiness to take offense. Only in the wilderness was everything serene, except for the Africans, who were enough to drive you crazy after a time. But he was patient and had learned to put up with a lot. He disliked white women and said openly that if he ever married it would be to "a black bint, who at least have no ideas about emancipation." He had never taken a woman on safari since the first and only experience of it he had

had, who happened to be a woman who rebuked him for not shaving and for wearing torn and stained clothing. She had been one of those women who had meant well, had wanted to see him looking better, because she had admired him.

"Well, that's the safari!" Gilligan had said after some sharp words with her. "It's finished. I'm taking you and your husband back, because I won't put up with it, missus. I won't put up with it. When you're out with me I'm boss and I don't want any words. Arguing and bad blood don't work in the bush. It's dangerous." This was one of his favorite expressions if anyone upset him or criticized him or argued with him on safari. "It won't work. I know the bloody bush and you've got to pull together in it, or you're done. I never let anyone argue with me."

"I hear you're hard to deal with," this American Muller, had written. "They say you're hard to get on with. Well, I'm no angel either, so it's O.K. with me. It's your elephant I want, that big one they tell me about."

Gilligan's elephant was well known to old-timers. He had an enlarged photograph of it in his shack out at Guyu. Only Gilligan knew where it lived. There was a story that Gilligan had run away from this elephant, a story that seemed to have something in it, but nothing was ever proved.

The elephant was the only thing that had ever managed to frighten Gilligan, even to terrify him, and he *had* run, after Pratt, his partner, had been picked up by it and smashed against a rock, and he had sacked the only witness of the scene, his tracker, at the end of the safari. He had never gone near an elephant since, but just now he needed every cent he could get his hands on, and had agreed to take Muller after it. Even though he was afraid, he was already excited about the safari.

This safari, quite illegal, barely planned, was more than an adventure for Gilligan, for while he loved the desiccated, sun-blasted silent wilderness in which this elephant lived, so far from civilization, he knew, worriedly, that he was letting circumstance, disguised as the American's money, take him to the elephant—his fear and his failure. He could not understand his own moods about the American, whom he had never met, but whom he was taking to the elephant.

'The bloody nerve of it,' Gilligan thought, hurling the empty beer bottle into the river. 'He likes it tough! Well, we'll see. He can find out about Africa, *my* Africa, and I'll bank the money.' "Write your own ticket," Muller had written. "I'll really pay you if I get that elephant."

It was all done very quietly, the arrangement for this illegal safari, and Gilligan talked exultantly aloud to himself about it by the river.

"Bloody game department!" He sneered at a crocodile sliding and sidling swiftly down the opposite bank. "A bunch of park keepers, that's all they are these days. They want uniforms and those little iron-tipped sticks for picking up people's entrance tickets into the bloody game reserves."

It had all changed so swiftly, Africa, in a rush of ideas and education and suburbia. They fed the lions on cold zebra now from the backs of trucks, and the lions had forgotten that they and men were traditional enemies. It made Gilligan bitter to think of it, when he remembered the old days of the ox wagons and the sea mail and the isolation, and the sense of personal greatness and uniqueness in the unknown bush country.

'Tough, are you?' he mused. 'Well, we'll see.' He almost hated Muller before he had even met him. He felt on his mettle, ready for anything. He was a little mad, and suspected it.

4

MULLER FOLLOWED Gilligan's carefully, almost conspiratorially, written instructions to the letter.

"Get into Guyu after dusk. Drive into the town. It's only a row of tin shacks. One of them is the Dewdrop Inn. Stop your truck outside and blow your horn three times. A fellow called Graig will come out and contact you. He's one of the old-timers and an old friend of mine. My tracker, Chongu, is with him. Graig will clue you up. I'll be waiting in my old camp by the Waso Larok River. Chongu knows it well. Chongu will guide you to my camp. *Say nothing about this to anyone. Don't trust anyone except Graig and Chongu.* I don't want anyone to know you're coming with me. This country's not what it was, but there are still a few left, like Graig. Give Graig fifty pounds and take it off my bill. He's hard up, an old-time hunter worth every other bastard who lives in this country these days. It's just a

30

place for clerks, ant-men, these days, but where we're going you'll see the Africa *that was* before the bureaucrats and their ant-men got hold of us." Gilligan's letter ended with another of the warnings which had been sprinkled through all his letters. *"Trust nobody if you want this elephant.* This country's full of people out to get me. Graig and Chongu are the only people who know about this safari. *Keep it that way.* I'm relying on you. *Say nothing to anybody."*

Muller laughed every time he reread any of Gilligan's letters. "A screwball," he said after reading the last letter. But he liked screwballs, knowing he was one himself, and the illicit feel of the whole thing attracted him. Although he had never been in Africa before, he was widely traveled and, like Gilligan, he hated administration and administrators. But he enjoyed civilization and considered he knew how to use it, and he was fond of adventure and tested himself all the time about his courage and his physical ability.

Graig came out into the warm darkness a few seconds after the third hoot of the horn. "Mr. Muller?" he asked.

He was a tiny, lean, gray-haired man with glittering blue eyes, wearing a white T-shirt and khaki shorts, his sun-darkened face ravaged looking in the glow of the headlights. He looked like an old army physical training instructor, fit and hard and spry. He jumped up onto the running board.

"Drive straight on," he commanded. "I'll guide you to where Gill and me live."

Muller drove slowly along the dirt road for about half a mile until Graig told him to turn left. He stopped the truck outside a long, low, grass-roofed shack with a sagging veranda lit by a white Petromax glare. He could see insects seething in frantic clouds around the fierce incandescence of the lamp. As he stopped the engine of the truck he heard yelping and wailing out on the dark plain.

"What the hell's that?" he asked.

"Hyenas, of course, and jackals," Graig said, looking sharply at him. "I banged down some zebra a couple of hours ago and they're having supper off them. Come on in and I'll give you a touch-up. I've got some first-class Nubian gin, made by an old Sudanese sergeant of mine. It'll knock the bloody fillings out of your back teeth. Leave your kit. You'll be pulling out in the dark anyway, so leave it. Here's Chongu." He shouted, *"Namna* bloody *gani,* Chongu?" to a thin, almost naked African who ran up with a hurricane lamp in his hand. *"Bwana yaku hapa natoka* bloody American *na wewe* sit on your arse all night? *Weka pombe tayari, tanganeze* bloody *meza.* Get cracking!"

They went into the shack's big living room where another Petromax poured blinding light onto what looked like a war museum, for the walls were covered with military trophies. Muller recognized Japanese helmets and swords, tunics stained with dried blood, Japanese army flags, all of them covering the wall between rhino heads and the horns of many species of antelope.

"They're all Gill's," Craig said. "He was in Burma with a special unit during the war. He killed a hell of a lot of Japs. Ah, the good old Nubian firewater." Chongu had appeared with glasses and a stone bottle on a tray.

"So you and Gilligan live here? That right? Been here

long?" Muller asked the question idly while Graig poured a glassful of the cloudy-looking gin for him.

"Yes, we're old pals," Graig said. "I'm the only bastard he could ever get on with." He looked into Muller's eyes. "He's not the easiest bloke on earth to get on with, you know."

"Neither am I," said Muller. He looked at the glass in his hand. "Will I live if I drink this?" he asked. "I mean will I die of cholera or something?"

"Nothing could live in that, chum," Graig said. "It'll kill any germ in sight." He watched while Muller took a big drink of it, as if waiting for choking noises. But Muller showed no signs of shock. He nodded appreciatively. "It's O.K.," he said, and drained the glass.

"You'll do, chum. You'll do," the old man said to him, a little disappointed. "Most people refuse to drink it. I never drink anything else nowadays. By the way, Gill said to ask you to leave a check with me for fifty quid. We're broke, you know. Times are tough. This bloody country's only for businessmen now. We've seen the best of it, as Gill would say."

"Fifty's no good if you're broke," Muller said. "I'll make it a hundred." He took a checkbook from the hip pocket of his suntan pants.

"No, fifty. Do what Gill says or there'll be a row," Graig replied. "I never argue with Gill. If he said fifty, it's fifty."

"O.K." Muller was irritated and he wrote the check out on the table. He was a tall, rangy, fair-haired man of about forty and when he looked at Graig his large hard gray eyes were ironic. "You think I'll really get that elephant?" he asked. "Is it really as big as they say?"

"Come and see the photograph. He's a big bastard, all right, don't worry about that." Graig narrowed his eyes and smiled, showing small, crumbled brown teeth. "Don't say anything," he went on, "but I think it was big enough for Gill."

"How do you mean?"

"This elephant is about the only bastard I know of that ever got away from Gill," said Graig, "human or animal. And he wasn't too keen to take you after it, either. It's the money. He needs it and he said you said to write his own ticket. I think it's a big bull all right. I've never seen it. Chongu has."

"You mean Gilligan was scared of it?"

"I never said that, chum," the old man replied, looking, almost glaring, into the tall American's eyes. "But I'd say this. He wouldn't break his leg going after it again if he weren't broke. It killed a fellow who was with Gill, a fellow called Pratt. I knew Pratt well. He was a nice chap, but he had a thing about being a dead shot with a camera. Take my tip, chum, you can't knock an elephant down with a camera. Smash him!" His voice rang in the room. "Smash him, chum! Hit him with a five hundred and when he falls onto his arse give him the other barrel. Can you shoot?"

"I can shoot," Muller said with a quiet reproof.

"What's the biggest thing you've shot?"

"Men," said Muller. "How about another shot of that liniment?" Graig poured him another glassful.

"You hungry?" Graig asked him.

"No. I want to get moving. Is that guy of yours ready? What's his name again?"

"Chongu. He's ready. He's been ready all day. You

were in the war? Is that what you meant, shooting men?"

"I've shot my quota," Muller told him seriously, with a look as if to say that would be enough on that subject. "This guy, Gilligan, he's hard to get on with, eh? What's the score?"

"The score?"

"Yeah, the score. What's his chip? What's he hard to get on with about?"

"It might be about anything," Graig replied. "You can never tell. He doesn't like arguing or anything like that. He's very particular about everything he does. Everything's got to be exact. You just get used to it after awhile. He's all right."

"Where's this photograph?"

"Oh, yes. Over here." He led the way to a photograph hanging in a black frame between a Japanese rifle and a stained Rising Sun flag, holding the lamp high to illuminate the shape of the huge elephant.

"Jeeze, he's big. You can say that again," Muller exclaimed. "Who took that photograph? He was pretty close."

"Pratt took it," Graig said. "Just before he got snatched up. Gill was covering him and something went wrong. Chongu went back later and found the camera." He paused. "Better not talk about any of it to Gill. He wouldn't like it. He won't even talk to me about it. Bad patch, you know." He laughed in a high wheezing, choking spasm. "We all have a bad patch somewhere in the background, eh?" Muller was looking at the picture of the enormous elephant, studying the long heavy tusks and the great ears pressed against the head and body.

"That's the one I want," he was saying. "It's going

to be some chore, getting the skin off that bull, but I'll do it. I've got two of the best skinners in this country with me, at least I was told they were. You reckon we'll get away with this O.K.? It's illegal, but has Gilligan got it all fixed?"

"Don't worry about that. But you said skinning. You mean you're going to skin this elephant?" Graig was laughing. "Any idea what you're taking on? Does Gill know about this?"

"Don't you worry," Muller replied, annoyed by Graig's laughter. "I've promised it to a museum. I've got a couple of cases of vodka in the truck. Like a snifter?"

"No thanks, Nubian for me. Well, O.K., it's all yours if you want to skin it. But you've got to shoot it first. You don't know that country up there where he's taking you. It's a bastard piece of country, I tell you. You won't feel like doing much skinning of an elephant at the end of it. But every man to his taste, eh?" He raised his head and began to yell in Ki-Swahili, "*Kama wewe* bloody *tayari*, Chongu, *Kuja na* bloody *sema. Na sakiyo? Bwana nataka kwenda sasa. Futa* bloody socks *yaku ju, na sakiyo?*"

"Chongu'll be ready now," he said. "Are you sure you wouldn't like a bite to eat?" Muller shook his head. "The moon's up so you'll have a fairly good trip," Graig went on. "Have you got boys and everything you need?"

"I've got everything except a piano," Muller said, holding out his hand. "See you."

"Good luck," Graig shook his hand. "And remember, don't cross Gill. Play along with him. He can be difficult."

"So can I," Muller said, tired of Graig's concern for

Gilligan's ways. "You make him sound like a really hard guy. But I'll manage."

"You've got to know his ways," Graig fretted as they went to the veranda. "Anyway, the best of luck. What are you using, by the way? Have you got a heavy rifle?"

"I've got the number you said, a five hundred, and a couple of others as well. Don't you worry, old-timer, I'll manage."

The moonlight was flooding the plains as he sat down at the steering wheel beside the sulky driver, whom he had forbidden to drive after studying his style during the first few miles.

Chongu climbed up onto the top of the loaded truck and sat among Muller's party of Africans. He was carrying a bow and a quiver of arrows and a long spear.

"You'll be all right with Gill and Chongu," Graig was saying across the revving of the engine. "They're a real pair together, those two. But one last word, watch Gill when you get to that elephant. That's between you and me." There was a strange expression in his eyes, almost fearful, as if he regretted what he had said, but had had to say it.

"Yeah? And then?" Muller took his cigarette out of his mouth and eyed the old man. "Why?"

"That's all." Graig grinned with his brown teeth. "Just that. Get him back whole, and you too. He's the best shot you ever saw, but he doesn't like that elephant. It's a bad elephant, that one." They looked at each other in silence for a few seconds and then Muller put the truck in gear. " 'By," he said.

5

THE TWO MEN got off to a bad start from the first few moments of their meeting.

It was dawn when Muller, with Chongu standing on the running board of the truck, drew up in Gilligan's camp. He could see Gilligan, naked to the waist in the first soft golden light, superintending the loading of camp equipment onto a truck.

"About time you got here, isn't it?" Gilligan shouted, turning from his inspection of his truck's tires. "I've been waiting for hours."

"How about some breakfast?" Muller called back. He got down from his truck. Gilligan gave him such a look that Muller hesitated with his ready right hand, but he thought he should go through with it, even after this belligerent and unexpected greeting. He held out his hand and said, "I'm Muller."

"I thought you must be," Gilligan said. His brown

38

chest was covered with ginger-and-gray hair. "And I'm Gilligan. And now we've got that over, there's some tea still in the pot. Get it down you quickly. We've got a hell of a long way to go, mister, and it's tough country. You've got a fortnight, you said in your letter, and you'll need it all if you want this elephant. Get your tea and I'll wait for you."

"Now wait a minute—" Muller said, smiling, but with angry eyes.

"Listen," Gilligan said forcefully, "this is a job we're on, not a picnic. I'm boss. I'm responsible for getting you there and back, and for finding you a special elephant you want. Right? I've been waiting for hours. We should have left long before dawn as it is. Now will you be a good chap and get your tea down you and follow me? Keep well back off my dust trail. The dust's murder for the first couple of hundred miles."

Gilligan had expected a fatter, smoother, more clerk-like American. Here, instead, was a tall, hard-looking, fit man with wide shoulders and big hands. They were both eying each other appraisingly.

"Listen," Muller said, "I'm no child. You hit the road. I'm having breakfast. Nothing in the goddam world ever prevents me from my having my breakfast when I want it. Nothing. You hit the road and I'll follow you."

Gilligan had not expected this. He seemed uncertain of his next words. "In this kind of country it's best to stick close together," he said. "Drink the tea. You won't die, you know. You'll get your meal later when I stop. But time's short and we've got to move if you want that elephant." But Muller had decided now that nothing would induce him to go without his breakfast, or more important, give in to Gilligan's stern commands. He kept cool and told Gilligan to go on and that he would join him later.

"Very well," Gilligan said, his blue eyes glittering with temper. "Very well. You saw Graig, I suppose, and spent the night drinking with him. Time's short, mister. We've got four days of driving across tough country to do. We're not in America now—"

"Listen, you hit the road, will you, and let me have my breakfast. And cool off. I don't go for this stuff, you see. Now you cool off and we'll get on O.K. Is that a deal?"

"I don't want a scene," Gilligan said menacingly. "I don't like them. You want your breakfast. Very well. Have your breakfast. But we can't go on like this if I've got to get you to that elephant and back in a fortnight. This isn't a bloody game reserve with park keepers and restaurants, you know. Have your breakfast then. I'm moving on." And he moved on. Muller watched his truck vanish into the bush ahead of a trail of thick yellow dust. His face wore an angry look and his mouth was shut tight.

'The guy's nuts,' he thought. 'I'll have to put a rope on him before long. No bastard is going to treat me that way.'

He could smell bacon frying. His cook, swift in sensing an atmosphere between the two white men, and guessing that Muller was somehow at fault, was anxious to help.

The more Muller thought of the strange scene between himself and Gilligan, between two strangers meeting for the first time in the wilderness, the more angry he became. And he was tired and wanted a sleep. But he felt challenged now, provoked and put on his mettle. "We're not in America now—" he said these words over to himself and seethed with anger. He decided to drive all out and catch up with Gilligan, be pleasant and casual, yet show that it was possible to have breakfast and to hustle and make up for time well lost.

It was two days, though, before he saw Gilligan again.

6

THE COUNTRY WAS FLAT HERE, a prairie of low gray scrub with tall thorn trees standing here and there, the distant ones shaking and quivering in the heat. The reddish-yellow earth threw up a glowing heat which filled the driving seat of the truck. Muller drove all day, with only a short break for a drink, and because he was hurrying, feeling he had to because of Gilligan's words, he stayed in a bad temper, sometimes cursing aloud as the heat increased and the sweat rolled off him. Ahead, through the dusty windshield, he could see the great prairie stretching for hundreds of miles.

He drove until nightfall, following the two tire tracks left by Gilligan, but he did not reach Gilligan. As the swift darkness began to fall across the riotous colors of the sunset, he decided to camp, and because he guessed that Gilligan had deliberately driven all out so as to teach him that this was work, not pleasure, he sat dumb with rage while Chongu and the servants set up his camp bed. He could not even complain to Chongu or the other three Africans, for he spoke no language known to them, though Chongu was pleased to say words in English like "tea, Bwana," and "fix him campu bed?"

Again the next day he drove all out across the wastes until he came into hilly and broken country on which the truck began to roll and bounce, until he became exhausted with the steady jolting and the muscular strain he had to use to endure it.

'The bastard's trying me out,' he was thinking, 'he's teaching me a lesson. The guy's nuts. Nuts. But we'll see later. No one does this to me and gets away with it. No one. And *I'm* the goddam client, treated like a dogface by a top sergeant. The guy's nuts. I'm supposed to get in to his camp eventually, finished, exhausted. Yeah? Difficult to get on with! Who's kidding? But so am I. I'll show this bastard who's difficult. The goddam nerve. The nerve.' He drove on, for hour after hour through the fierce sun glare, and all the time he brooded about Gilligan.

Muller was one of those men who watched himself all the time, studying himself and looking for motives and drives and hints of failure. He set himself a high standard, yet was not complicated or harassed by living, and this high standard was about courage, in action as well as in opinion, and about integrity and the right to be himself while not crowding his fellows. Across this, though, fell a shadow of his driving personality, and of his pleasure in being himself, fit and reasonable and courageous. He liked to be liked and to be handled warmly, because everything was fine then. He knew he was likable, despite his aggressiveness. But if somebody wanted it tough, he was always ready, like now. He considered that it was only with people like himself, reasonable and well-integrated people, that he was at his best, that he felt at ease. That was why he was putting together a picture of Gilligan now as he gripped the steering wheel of the lurching, surging truck and drove it carefully over the rocks. It was a picture of a man who had lived on his own for years, opinionated, vain, stupid and, he had good reason to believe, shifty from failure.

Take those words spoken by Graig about this guy, Gilligan, and this elephant. He had obviously meant that Gilligan had left that elephant well alone after it had killed Pratt. Guys who did not go through with a mess to the very end usually finished up like this Gilligan, full of scar tissue covering self-inflicted wounds. The more he thought of his strange scene with Gilligan in that camp at dawn the more sinister it appeared to become, as if he and Gilligan were now involved in a pilgrimage Gilligan had put off for years. 'And he's mad,' Muller thought. 'Those eyes, and the way he spoke to me as he'd known me for years and didn't approve of me. The bastard's driving all out and I'm driving all out after him, trying to catch up. What *is* this? I mean what am I doing it for? I'll talk to this guy. I'll say my piece. Because this is crazy. This is a waste of time. I mean I want my breakfast and he says no and I disobey him and he clears off to hell out of it and here I am driving all out after him. The stupid, goddam weirdo, ought to be in a nut house, that's where.'

Sweat rolled into Muller's eyes, salty and stinging, and he wiped it away swiftly, his wet hand flying back to the twisting steering wheel. 'He wasn't kidding when he

said the country was tough. I'll say that.' He had been in
heat before, floundered in the hot swamps of Guadalcanal
during the war, been dried out and scorched, but this sun
above him now was like an oven blazing on top of the
steel roof above his head.

"*Iku mutu, Bwana,*" the driver sitting beside him said
suddenly, pointing ahead with his pursed lips. Muller
looked through the dusty windshield and saw a man
about five hundred yards ahead, standing on the plain,
waiting. It was Jama, Gilligan's Somali gunbearer, and
he waved as Muller's truck approached him.

It was a great relief for Muller to hear Jama speaking
in English as he braked the truck beside him and leaned
out of the cab.

"Bwana Gilligan sack me," Jama said, smiling slowly,
but his black eyes were as hard as two stones. "Very hot
man. He got hot, shouting, nothing go right. Insult me.
Call me bloody fool." Jama began to act out the scene,
waving his hands. "He say, 'Somali no bloody good.
Where you put bullets for big rifle? Where you put
lamp? Lamp broke now. You broke lamp.' I say, 'No
break lamp.' He say, 'Bloody liar. Bloody fool.' I say,
'Not bloody liar. Not bloody fool.' He go hit me. No one
hit me. *No one!*" Jama had begun to shout, his eyes burning. "I get knife out and hold like this. He stop. 'No one
hit me,' I say. He say, 'I kill you, bloody fool, take knife
to me.' 'No one hit me,' I say. 'Right,' he say. 'Finish. All
finish.' He throw my references on floor. He throw my
box off truck. He throw some money on floor. Finish.
He get in truck and go." Jama waved his fists in the air,
his teeth bared, hysterical with rage. "He bloody madman, this *Bwana Pumbavu*. He hate Somali mans because

Somali mans not slave like kneeling down for fist. He bloody madman this *Pumbavu*."

"You're hired," Muller said. "I knew the guy was nuts. He should be in the nut house. Get aboard. You want a drink?"

Muller lifted a bottle of vodka out of a water-sodden canvas bucket hanging on a hook where the breeze could get at it.

"Somali mans no drink *tembo*," Jama said, smiling. He was quivering with the emotions he had evoked during his scene. "I drink water or camel milk." He drank from a water bottle handed down by one of the Africans on the truck.

"You want a job?" Muller asked.

"I no work with *Bwana Pumbavu*. I no want Bwana Gilligan. He hate Somali mans."

"You can work for me. Get aboard. How far ahead is Bwana Gilligan?"

"He drive fast. Very fast. He stop to make *kojoa* and drink but no camp. He go fast. Stop only make piss and drink. He very angry all the time."

"O.K. You're hired." That would really annoy Gilligan, his hiring Jama. Muller was shocked at this jettisoning of a man in the middle of a burning wilderness, far more shocked than Jama to whom wilderness was no problem. Jama's passion was centered on the insult he had received. He was glad to be away from Gilligan. Only a slave would crawl back onto Gilligan's truck after their scene together. Even if Gilligan had not left him in the wilderness Jama would have thought little of staying there, for he was nearer to his own tribal territory than he had been three days ago.

He smiled at Muller, thanking him. "All right, Bwana," he said, "I work for you. But Bwana Gilligan, he make *fitina* for this. He be angry see me with you."

"Great," Muller said. "Jump up. We're off." Again he began the struggle with the truck as it started on its journey over the rocks. It was nearly sundown when he saw the smoke of a campfire rising like a thin blue thread into the reddening sky ahead. Half an hour afterward he could see Gilligan's truck.

"Right, you bastard," Muller said aloud. "You picked the wrong Joe this time. It's the elephant I want, not you, but we must sort a few things out first. People aren't animals."

7

MULLER GOT DOWN from his truck full of purpose, looking grim, his opening words rehearsed several times.
"Look, Gilligan," he was going to say, "what the hell goes
on? I'm steaming mad and I want an explanation. What
are you trying to do?" He was completely disconcerted
by Gilligan's friendly smile. Gilligan was standing with
his hands on his hips, a picture of good will and friendli-
ness, saying, "You're pretty good, man. That was fast
going you made. Great. We've torn off a good strip of
the trip now and can relax."

After a momentary hesitation Muller, never one to hold
a grudge for long, thought, 'Right. I'll take it from here.
The guy's nuts. O.K. But now he's O.K. I want to knock
him flat, but no. Dig the friendship, though, and the big
smile.' He had to seek fast for new words. When they
came they were not as good-natured as he had hoped. He
was too angry, and had worked himself up too often in
the long hours of silence in the cab of his truck.

"Anyone ever hint to you that you were eccentric?" he asked, smiling thinly to give it a suggestion of possible friendly banter.

"We're all eccentric, mister," Gilligan said, still smiling. "With me you can knit or you can sing hymns, do anything you like, I'm not funny that way. But when it comes to moving or to the routine, I like it my way. You do it my way and you'll get your elephant and be back in time to catch your aircraft." And behind his words and his smile was the command again, the easy determination to be boss, and this seemed so needless and childishly inadequate to Muller that all his willingness to forget what had happened vanished in fresh anger.

"Listen," he said, "I'm not used to being pushed around or catered for like I was ten years old. Get it? You may have the best intentions in the world, you may have everything organized, but I don't go for it that way. And I'll tell you something else. That was a lousy thing to do to your Somali guy, throwing him off your truck and leaving him on his ass in the sand. I'm paying for this safari and I have some ideas about it, too, I mean how I want to see it run. This isn't a chain gang or a stockade. You want to change your mind about your Somali and take him back? If not I'm keeping him."

"You *what?*" Gilligan was astounded by these last words. They were out of sight of Muller's truck, standing under a high green-boled thorn tree. "You picked that impudent bastard up off the road, you mean? What right have you got to interfere with my servants? In this country we white men back each other up, mister. We don't do this kind of thing. He's sacked and I sacked him. *I'm* the judge of who works on this safari. If I think a man's no good he goes. That's my way and don't you interfere with it." He was trying not to shout, but his voice was hard and urgent. He was glaring into Muller's eyes, both fists clenched by his sides, outraged by the way his decision about Jama had been undone by this stranger.

"Will you quit sounding off like a top sergeant, Gilligan?" Muller said, some menace in his voice. "I won't goddam well put up with it. Now quit it or there'll be trouble."

"Trouble?" Like a buffalo scenting threat, and quickly pugnacious with it, Gilligan thrust his head forward at Muller. "Are you threatening me?" he went on, as if unable to believe what he had heard.

"Take it slow and we'll get somewhere," Muller told him. "Quit this mastermind, superman stuff, and we'll get on. But don't upset me any more because I've had all I'm taking. This is kid stuff, this shouting and yelling. Now cool off. I'm going to have a drink. Cool off, and if you feel like it you can join me. It's vodka. Nice cold vodka. That's what I want, vodka, not playing kids. I'm supposed to be enjoying myself, on safari. Remember?"

Gilligan, calmer now, but full of warning and controlled anger, said, "It won't do. It won't do. I'm not having that Somali in my camp." He turned and walked off toward his truck.

In the few minutes with Muller, Gilligan had experienced an unusual sensation, a feeling of wanting to draw back from his position, for here was a personality which disturbed him, a man whose attitude seemed to be backed by a hard and combative personality. There was a sort of challenge in everything Muller had done and said in their two short meetings, and for two days he had gone over the scene about Muller's breakfast, and he had been using his will on himself, been thoughtful as well as furious. In solitude he knew once again that he did not like "clients," and that as someone had once knowingly remarked to him, "Your trouble, Gill, is that you hate your bloody clients because they're rich and you're working for them." He had never forgotten that remark, one of those remarks which frame what a man may suspect about himself for a long time and which confirms many half-admitted suspicions.

He knew that he liked to dominate and to be admired, and to show efficiency, coolness, strength, courage, and, most of all, to be proved right in the end. Again and again he had bitterly quarreled with people, a good many of whom had not wanted to quarrel at all, and he sat down on a rock now and smoked, and fretted in surges of anger. He was not going to be put down, to be bested, by this American, and it was plain that this American was all out to have his own way and had been *thinking* about it. He knew that Muller had been thinking about him and had taken a dislike to him. That was a mistake, to take that attitude so readily because he had not been able to sit down, like one of the ant-men, and have his breakfast. Gilligan did not care about meals when on safari. At night, yes, have everything then, meat and drink and talk, but in the day one went flat out to the objective, particularly with "clients" who were liable to laze about and want baths and lie on their beds in the shade reading books. He had had all that so often, and he could not put up with it. Action. That was the purpose of safari, that was the thing to move to. Action. But this Muller could eat his breakfast and travel all out as well, and look fresh and unperturbed at the end of it, 'AND flout my bloody orders.' He had picked up that Somali and then had the cheek to criticize him, Gilligan, for sacking the arrogant bastard. Gilligan got up from the rock, his teeth clenched. He had never had anything like this happen before, and he must act. That Somali was sitting in the camp, triumphant, waiting to see what he, Gilligan, was going to do now.

'Do? Do? I'll show you, boy.' He strode to the camp. 'This thing has got to be finished, once and for all. I should have got down to it right away.' But he had not wanted to face it. He had gone away to think about it, and had only just seen that he had done so. Was he slipping? Was he windy? A feeling of crisis swept over him, even though he knew that it was hardly likely that Muller would have passed by a man stranded in the desert. Never mind, Muller was new here and did not know the form, and the form was this, that what one white man did, no matter what it was, in the bush, the other one backed him up, especially about face and position where the *watu* were concerned. The *watu* knew the form and when one of them was sacked, that was it, and that was all about it. It was a very personal thing, master and man.

By the time he reached Muller, who was lying on his camp bed under a tree, Gilligan was in the mood for a fight. Despite his temper, though, he knew that once again he had begun to go wrong, had started something and must finish it. But it had to be done, for no matter how he looked at it he was in the right. He was the boss and he knew this world of wilderness like the back of his hand, and he wanted to be respected, to be left to be himself, in charge and worthy of it, for that was what he was, worthy and able. He stood over Muller, who looked up at him and said, "Have a snort. There's a glass there on the chair. Like vodka?"

"About this Somali I sacked," Gilligan began, his face sullen, and immediately Muller shot up off his back and said in an exaggerated cry of despair, "Oh, Jeeze, not again, not *again*. Forget it, will you? Relax. Take your badge off and have a drink. I'm trying to goddam well enjoy myself, pal. Now will you let a guy enjoy himself?" He was playing but serious.

"It's a serious matter, Muller," Gilligan said, ignoring Muller's invitation to lightheartedness and fun. "I'm not having him in my camp. He's dangerous and I've sacked him. I know these people and you don't. Now don't dig your heels in. There's nothing to get worked up about—"

"Dig *my* heels in?" Muller laughed and tossed the rest of his vodka down his throat. "Are you kidding? I'm easy, pal. All I want is to enjoy myself, and I'll tell you something." He looked determined as he met Gilligan's cold stare. "All you have to do to enjoy yourself is to want to do it. You dumped that guy in the desert." He waved his hand. "Don't give me that about how no native minds that kind of thing, it's their life and so on. I know all that crap. Now relax. I've taken him on. You won't have any need to have anything to do with him. Now for Jeezes sake will you sit down and have a drink with me?"

"He's got to go," Gilligan said. "This is my safari and he was engaged by me, and I've sacked him—" his voice rose "—and that's my order, and I want it obeyed, and I don't want you interfering, Muller. You want an elephant and I'll take you there to get it. But everything else is my affair. Have you got that?"

"Now wait a minute, pal." Muller stood up and faced Gilligan, and both of them, extroverts who had brought themselves up in muscle and thoughts about courage, men who had to live their masculine dreams, were measuring each other up for size, strength, will, two of the permanent, wild, pioneer boys of time. It was Muller who first knew that they were alike, that they should never have met like this in the very place to prove such things as who was toughest, who was bravest, and he had to stop himself from laughing as he realized it while looking into Gilligan's blue eyes. He was luckier than Gilligan, he thought, for Gilligan was more frightened about himself than he, Muller, was. "A bad patch," he thought, remembering Graig's words.

"Make your mind up, Gilligan," Muller was saying. "He's staying with me. I've given him a job, and that's that. Now let's not be goddam fools and fight about your Somali. Because I'm telling you that's what we're going to do if you go on. You do what you want, O.K. You did it. You dumped him in the sand on his ass. I do what I want too. I picked him up and took him on. Fine. Now, I'm asking you, will you have a drink with me, or does this kind of thing go on all the time, this power struggle?"

There it was, you see, the challenge. He had known it all along, as soon as he had set eyes on Muller during the breakfast incident. Gilligan was wavering, for Muller's sardonic eyes were making the situation look ridiculous, yet the fact remained that Jama was dangerous, had pulled a knife on him, and had been sacked and was now protected by this fellow who knew nothing about Africa.

"He drew a knife and threatened me with it," Gilligan said, incensed to hear himself actually explaining things, as if he must do this so as to be able to run his own camp. "Nobody does that to me, especially a black. This isn't New York. There are no courts and magistrates down here. I'll tell you something. If I'd been on my own when he drew that knife I'd have shot the bastard on the spot—" he smiled—"but I knew you were coming along behind. You get that Somali out of this camp. He's a bad one. And remember this. I run this camp and if I don't like any black in it out he goes." And he weakened then, reached out his hand and said, "Thanks, I will have that drink," yet it made Muller uncertain about the next move, that sudden gesture from Gilligan after the hard talk.

He poured a vodka for Gilligan, saying, "You'll have to make your mind up, pal. Jama's staying with me. I've taken him on. It's too bad, but *I'm* wayward too, pal. Think it over. You're in the wrong. He drew a knife, but only because you were going to hit him. Right?"

"I never explain my decisions to anyone. And I'm not going to start now. You're interfering. I know you mean well, but you're wrong. Back down. I won't think any the less of you for backing down."

"Yeah?" Muller laughed at the cool way Gilligan had given him permission to back down. "You're knocking yourself out, pal, with this struggle for power thing. Forget it. I'm asking you as a favor to forget it." His voice changed now. "Because if you won't you're going to find me to be the meanest bastard you ever came across. I like it friendly and reasonable, but you don't seem to want it that way. You go out of your way looking for fights. Why? I'm willing to forget the whole thing if you are." He said it again. "If *you* are."

"Really?" Gilligan needed a little time to think. "You're

making a big issue out of this, Muller. I'm not used to it. I don't take this kind of thing, you know. I've explained my position. I've sacked a servant." He became astounded suddenly at what he was putting up with, at the way he was talking himself into a losing position. He almost shouted, "And he's got to go. D'you hear? He's got to leave this camp. My reputation depends on it. He's got to go."

"Your reputation?"

"I'm not going to discuss it any further. Either you get Jama out of here or I do, but he's going out of this camp."

"Your reputation? How do you mean? I don't give a goddam about your reputation, Gilligan. To me it's a simpler thing than that. You threw a guy out on his ass, in the middle of a desert, and I've taken him on. And he's staying with me. You mean the other Africans will think you've knocked yourself out for nothing if Jama stays on here, they'll think you've lost face? It's your own goddam fault if they do. You've no right to throw a guy into the desert and leave him there. That's more important than your reputation."

"You don't live here. You're an American, dashed in on a trip, and you start preaching about the rights of man. I have to live here. I don't want to hear your views on the rights of man." He pushed his head forward with the vehemence of what he went on to say. "If you want to be a missionary, if you want to do something for the oppressed, then get back to America and fight for the right of your Negroes to be Americans. You have a bloody nerve coming here and trying to upset things because you think you represent democracy. I won't put up with it. I won't."

"The elephant's the thing that matters, not Jama," Muller said hotly. "That's what we're here for, to get that goddam elephant. Now will you quit this bitching about Jama and shake hands?"

"Don't be ridiculous. *Shake hands!*" Gilligan was embarrassed by the suggestion, almost recoiling, his brows tight with frown. "Don't be stupid. There's nothing to be dramatic about. I'm in command of this camp and that's it, and I won't be interfered with—"

"In *command*, eh?" Muller laughed angrily. "*Command!* O.K. Have your dream, general. But *I'm* paying. I'm paying for everything, and you need the dough. Right? Ashamed? Think it's a disgrace to need American dough or something? Is that it? Is that what's sticking in your craw? I've read about you guys. You need the dough but you want to cut the guy's throat who hands it out. Don't take me that way, pal. I'm grown up. See? I'm friendly. You're determined to make this into a big thing about how an American with no culture, no old ruins and no tradition, comes rushing in and gets everything wrong and needs to be shown what's what. That kind of crap makes me tired, Gilligan. How about this elephant? You want to go after it? You really *want* to go after it, or are you trying for some reason of your own to break this party up? You want to turn back for some reason, and looking for a reason? Is that it?"

There was an unmistakable suggestion about something in the way Muller had spoken these words, in the look in his eyes, that startled Gilligan.

"What are you getting at?" he asked sharply, too sharply, he thought when he heard his words.

"Getting at? Why? Should I be getting at something?"

It was a strange and anxious moment, this, and Gilligan wanted to draw back, but he was stung by Muller's words and he wanted to know a little more, but not too much, did not want to hear any of his own suspicions voiced.

"Explain what you're getting at," he commanded.

"You're all excited," Muller said, realizing he had revealed, without meaning to, too many of his secret thoughts. He had just realized that he was moving toward a position in which he was going to accuse Gilligan of being frightened of that elephant, of having a thing about it and about the death of that fellow, what was his name, Pratt. He had wanted to wound Gilligan, but now he was sorry for him, for he knew what it was to have that sleepless mania about courage and "How'm I doing today? Ready to die? Take on anything? Or am I slipping?" He had had to fight all that during the war, for he had been afraid all the time, and had worked on it, drilled himself into one of the finest killers in the Pacific. He still dreamed about it all, but only if something had gone wrong with the day, say if someone had not liked him when he wanted to be liked. He knew he was too sensitive, too afraid and anxious about people. But not with this slob here. He was beginning to hate Gilligan. "You're all excited," he said. "Cool off." Gilligan was quivering in front of him, almost comically had Muller not had to watch him tensely, ready to parry a fist maybe, and then over with the old right cross to that stupid goddam head. For a few seconds they stood there, breathing heavily and looking malevolently into each other's eyes, and then

Gilligan said, "Think it over, Muller, think it over," turned on his heel, and walked back to his bed under one of the thorn trees.

'He folded,' Muller thought exultantly, primitively, 'he folded. The bastard's chicken after all.' And he was sorry for Gilligan. He was sure Gilligan wanted as much money as he could get for this safari, and was sure too that Gilligan never wanted to go near that elephant again, but was going to make himself do it. What looked like a trip through the bush was something else, he was certain of it, was a crusade to a wounded place in Gilligan's memory, that part of a man's archives where the simplest and oldest tradition of all, physical courage, was jumbled and unreadable.

'Maybe I'm cooking it all up,' Muller mused over another vodka, but he thought not. He was fond of amateur psychology and he knew all the words like "overcompensation," "power drives," "total recall," and "sick." 'The guy's sick,' he thought. 'Sick.' From then on he began to behave as though he were dealing with a sick man. He decided that what Gilligan needed was to face everything, talk it over, unload, and get integrated again. 'This guy's suffering hell,' he thought, sorry for Gilligan again, 'and he needs help. He's sick. That's why he can't get on with anybody. He's wounded.' He knew he was right, but he was shrewd enough to know that few Europeans thought in modern American terms about these things, at least not of Gilligan's generation. That generation liked to bottle everything up and be stout fellas and keep a stiff upper lip.

'I wonder what *did* happen about this elephant?' he thought, and he wanted to know everything after that.

8

ONE OF THE REASONS Gilligan did not like people was
that he generally had trouble with them, unless they were
Africans, most of whom did what he told them. He
usually felt disaster coming, usually knew when things
were going wrong between himself and other men. But
this time, with Muller, he felt more uneasy than usual,
felt as if somehow he were being driven into a corner, and
as if a dangerous situation was being built all around him.
He did have keen intuition about situations, and it had
often been a help to him in the bush with a wounded
buffalo or rhino. He let his nerves work for him at times
and just now they were wide awake and worried. This
Jama thing—Jama being protected by this fellow, Muller.
It was dangerous. He rather admired Muller for standing
up to him the way he had done, while hating him for it as
well. He was, though, feeling distraught about the way
he had walked away from Muller instead of going through
with the thing to the very end. And he knew he had

walked away because his mind had begun to teem with speculations about what Muller might have heard about this Pratt business. There was no doubt that Muller had been getting at the Pratt business. That was why he had walked away. That was one thing. But Jama was another.

He went to see Jama, found him sitting under a tree in the moonlight not far from the campfire, and called him aside. They had their talk about twenty yards from the camp and Gilligan tried to put the best face on it that he could in the circumstances. Yet he was in a state of tension and even foreboding, for here he was again in retreat, being hard with Jama but without having his heart in it. Had he had his heart in it he would have given Jama five minutes to disappear from this camp. Instead, he made threats, painted an arrangement that would suit him, all of it designed to show him as a boss who had had second thoughts, and who could afford to have them, as boss. He had to work to convince Jama, though, and he knew it, for Jama was a Somali, swift-brained, sensitive, and hard to fool.

Jama was solemn, grave, as he faced Gilligan in the fierce moonlight which silvered their faces.

"This American is *m'geni*, a stranger," Gilligan began. "He does not know the customs. He means well. That is why you are still here, you see. Because he does not know the *dasturi*, the customs of the country. I have no time for a *shauri* just now, no time to explain these things to him. We are going after elephant and there is little time. But I don't want you near me. Do you hear? Keep out of my way. Stay far away from me. No one has ever shown me a knife before and got away with it—"

"I drew knife protect myself. I am Somali mans. We cannot let men hit us, Bwana," Jama began to explain,

angered still by Gilligan, but anxious for a quiet life. But
he understood why Gilligan resented having him around
the place, for men like Gilligan were like himself, proud
and willing to go to great lengths to maintain the right to
be proud. So he closed his mouth and listened when
Gilligan, like some chieftain, raised his hand for silence
and stared at him with threatening eyes.

"So you can stay with this American until we get to
the Janali Ganjo River. Then you cross it and head for
your own people, and never let me see you again, because
I tell you this, Jama, I am a man of the old times, of
somani, when if someone challenges my authority I will
kill him before stepping backward. You know that way,
don't you, like the Somalis with their enemies." He smiled
at the flicker of pride in Jama's eyes at this appraisal of his
race's virtue. "So I don't need to say any more to you.
Do I?" Gilligan went on. "But remember it. Keep out of
my way. I am done with you. The American was sorry
for you." He laughed. "He thinks you will die, as *he*
would, if left in the bush." Jama laughed too, treacher-
ously, at Muller's innocence, but Gilligan would not
allow that beginning of thaw to go on. He silenced it
immediately. "Now get out, Jama, and stay out of my
way, and when we come to the Janali Ganjo, vanish.
Vanish. Na fahumu amri yangu?"

Jama nodded, and said that he understood the order.
He was raging, and he admired Gilligan, a man of princi-
ple and will, and he knew too that nothing would give
so much pleasure to Gilligan as to kill him, and his own
fierce heart itched with a similar wish and he and Gilligan
understood each other well.

'It's a pity I couldn't get on with him,' Gilligan was

thinking. He admired the Somalis, but he could never bring himself to live with them on their terms. They were too proud. He watched Jama walk back to the camp with his long easy thin-legged nomad's stride, and he thought, 'I don't like any of this caper at all. I don't like it.'

He sat down to supper with Muller and was silent while the American talked about his journey to East Africa as if nothing had happened between them. And then, after listening for some time to what Muller thought of Nairobi, he interrupted.

"You can keep Jama," he said. "I've seen Jama and told him you can keep him, for now. But I've told him to keep out of my way." Perhaps it was a wish to be friendly that made him lean forward, knife and fork in his big hard hands, and say, "I've never let a black get away with it like that before. Maybe I'm softening up." He smiled sardonically at Muller.

"Maybe you are," Muller said. "You can knock yourself out with this prestige thing. You did right, pal. No harm in softening up."

"I told Jama you don't know the customs here, and that I'm playing along for that reason."

"Don't feel bad about it."

"I'm not feeling bad about anything," Gilligan said angrily. "I'm bloody well telling you why that bastard is still here, that's all."

Muller rolled his eyes upward in the moonlight, which so upset Gilligan, who was in a strange state of anxiety as it was, that he left the table and did not appear again.

'I'll have to undo this guy,' Muller thought. 'This is a real case. Like that top sergeant I had after Okinawa who hated my guts because I was braver than he was.'

9

Hoping to surprise muller and to keep his own end up, Gilligan got up especially early the next morning and began to move silently, calling quietly to Aganaza to roll his bed up and get the truck ready to go. It was still dark. The truck was ready in half an hour, and while there was still half an hour to go before the false dawn, that glimmer of steely gray light, Gilligan went to call Muller, to stand fully dressed over him and say, "Hey," jokingly, "rise and shine. We've got to get moving," but seriously, not jokingly.

Muller was not there, nor was his bed. He could see Muller's truck across the clearing beyond the huge glowing bed of the dying campfire. He went across to it. He did not know what to say when he saw Muller sitting at the wheel of his truck, fully dressed, smoking a cigarette, his feet up on the dashboard.

"Hiya," Muller said, smiling at him. "You certainly

take your time. I've been sitting here for half an hour waiting to move. We've only got a fortnight. Remember?" He spoiled it by breaking into loud laughter, and adding, "Jeeze, you look like somebody handed you a hot plate."

"This is ridiculous, childish!" Gilligan exclaimed.

"Are *you* kidding? I heard you creeping about, pal. I knew right away what you were doing. You were knocking yourself out all over again, pulling a fast one on me. Then you were going to come over to my bed and start that breakfast thing again, and feel great all day. Childish? As soon as you let up, pal, I'm your friend. But quit the push-ups. I can do as many push-ups as you can. Now, how about being a sport and having a laugh? You've got to admit I was on the ball this morning. Hey?"

"It's ridiculous," said Gilligan. A feeling of almost hysterical antagonism for Muller was getting hold of him. He wanted to drag Muller out of the truck and knock him down. It was as if Muller was driving him to continual contest, although he knew it was all his own fault.

"I thought you'd laugh, pal. I thought you were a sport," Muller said. "I knew what you were up to so I got in first, and now you look as if you'd like to have a duel with me. It's crazy." Even he, though, felt worried by what they were doing, by what was going on between them. He had known that Gilligan would not be amused by this defusing of his surprise, his new effort to be in first, but he had done it with a kind of glee. He knew too that they were fatal people to be together in this kind of situation. He was trying not to hate Gilligan, and it was hard.

"I'll lead the way," Gilligan said. "The country gets

rockier after a few more miles. Have you filled your radiator? It's tough going."

"Listen," Muller said, provoked again. "Cut this boy scout thing. I've driven in tougher country than this. I've been driving since I was a kid. I know about radiators."

"Don't get worked up now," Gilligan was playful, and Muller knew he had been unreasonable, and that it was a perfectly ordinary thing for Gilligan to ask about his radiator, and yet nothing was ordinary between Gilligan and himself. Everything was somehow loaded, mined, and usually ended up by being about who was the best man of the two. Quite pleased with himself now, Gilligan went to his truck. As it ground away out of the camp site the first sunlight welled up in a quivering sea of red flame on the horizon, turning all the thorn trees into glowing candelabra. Muller let Gilligan get well ahead, until his long rising twisting dust plume was drifting like reddish smoke across the bush. Then he moved forward onto the rocky path and began once again the struggle with the steering wheel of the bucking, rolling truck.

It was a hard, sweating day, so hard and tiring that Muller wondered at times if he did want that elephant after all. When they stopped at midday for a bite to eat and some beer with it, Muller sat in silence, tired, and depressed by the thought of the days of journey ahead, and Gilligan watched him covertly, pleased at this first sign of physical humility.

'Some of the spring's gone out of him,' he thought. 'Very nice too. In a couple more days he'll be eating out of my hand.'

10

Sitting in the truck, in one of those reveries brought on by monotonous travel in wilderness, Gilligan thought over his life and about the way it had passed by, like a fast river, and how it seemed to be going faster all the time. Suddenly you were sixty. Suddenly you were dead. It was no use saying, "I've enjoyed my life." He wanted to live forever, for no matter about all his troubles, usually caused by people getting into his life, he loved being alive and appreciated it all the time. And there had been peaks in it too, one of which he was thinking of now, for while he hated governments and administrations, knowing they brought death to the simple and the free, he liked administrators like Pratt. He always tried to think of Pratt up to the time of the elephant, and then fought to switch off, but the elephant always walked up into the reverie and stood there, screaming, with blood on its tusks, and then he ran again. Why, why, why had he run? He rammed his foot down on the accelerator in his pain, staring ahead through the windshield with stricken eyes, like a man just hit by a bullet.

He had been thinking of how he and Pratt had gone up to Lolbuki in the old days, when Pratt had been stocking the mountain streams with trout, which for Pratt had been a holy and sacred work. "One day when the descendants of these tribes are driving out here in their cars for a picnic, with their fishing rods, they'll say, 'I wonder who put these trout here?' providing they know, of course, that there weren't any here until I came, and someone'll say, 'Somebody called Bwana Pratt!' Now, I ask you, Gill, could a fellow want a better memorial than that, Africans smoking pipes, wearing flannels, and fishing quietly and happily for my trout? Could he? I get pleasure whenever I think of it."

"You're trying to get at me," Gilligan used to say when Pratt drew these pictures of the future, for Pratt knew his views, knew he wanted Africa to stay the way it was, innocent and wild and with only white men like Pratt and Gilligan in it.

"How dreadfully egotistical you are, Gill," Pratt would say. "Do you remember that I'm here to get people ready to enjoy this marvelous country one day. It's no use acting the old settler with me. That's the job I'm here for. *You're* here to live like a savage and grow more and more morose. You're becoming impossible." Pratt knew all about the strange manias Africa put into men. And he knew he had his own, and what they were.

Pratt was the best friend he had ever had. Pratt had great respect for him, for his knowledge of the Africans and for his bush skills. Pratt had been one of those unforgettable English individuals, eccentric, with charm, and without violence or smallness in his nature. If only there had been about six administrators like Pratt, and NO government, everything could have gone on forever, for whatever Pratt might say about the future, he believed in the native customs being allowed to wither slowly if they wanted to, while those that were strong could stay and grow into other things one day. He used to say, "We're kicking Africa in the stomach too often. It's on it's knees."

Why, why had he let him down that day among the roasting boulders on that forest edge, seen him whirled up and swung like a club against the rocks, uttering one long cry which sometimes brought Gilligan up sweating out of his sleep after a tiring or oppressive day. Yes, yes. He had turned after missing with his right barrel, missing because of fear, while Pratt, eccentric, unafraid, utterly reliant upon his friend's impeccable shooting, had bent absorbed, and certainly thrilled with what was looming in the frame of his camera, as the enormous bull came on. It should have fallen. Then there would have been a bottle of beer, and years more of friendship. Instead he had seen Pratt, with his gray hair and gold-rimmed glasses, snatched up and smashed like a fruit against a rock. What had possessed him, a normally courageous man, to turn and run, and run far, trying to catch up with his fleeing tracker? But as soon as that right barrel missed, the tracker, with those keen senses of his, had known that it was all too late now, and the thing to do was not to be there, to go, and fast.

'He knew I hated elephant. He knew I was never easy with them. He remembered that time down at Ngorongoro years ago when I shivered and he saw me, when that cow came out of the forest and I wasn't ready, wasn't expecting her. And I let her go. Tusks like knitting needles. But he saw me. Yes, the bastard saw me. And then I missed with Pratt there standing all gone with his camera about the bull coming, best picture ever taken, etcetera, for Gill couldn't possibly miss. Best bloody shot in Africa. Sweating, though, all the time. Yes, sweat pouring off. I did it all that first time when I was raw, before the locusts came when I was playing at farming and the elephants came and it was night and out I rushed, no clue at all, thinking all you had to do was have a rifle and shoot.'

He stamped down harder on the accelerator, as once more he began to go over the history of Gilligan and the elephants. He was terrified of them, and had been so ever since he had run in blind fear after wounding his first one, through bush, among trees, over rock, in darkness, through maize fields, with the screaming beast on his heels gone mad with rage. Darkness, yes. He had made the river safely, the opposite bank from his shack, and had dived into it in the darkness, unknowing, swimming like a madman across it, to safety, and had lain as if dying from fear and exhaustion in the reeds on the other bank, while the Africans yelled in the night, not knowing, mercifully, how the Bwana had obeyed that terrific force, the longing to live, instead of standing and finishing what he should never have begun in darkness.

Everything that came afterward, lion, leopard, buffalo, rhino, he had shot it down, each one a contest with his eye and his nerve, and he had shot hundreds of them, but he could never rest about the elephant, and never face them; never managed to beat them. That was why he was here now, on this rocky path, he knew it, as if all those years ago were yesterday and he was taking up the chase after a night's sleep. "Should have gone back that day, and gone through with it, died if necessary." He often thought, as he thought now, in a kind of spasm of self-hatred. "Should have died if I couldn't make it." Elephant obsessed him. "I never shoot elephant," he had said many times, wanting it passed on, repeated, taken into the white folklore. "I'm too fond of them. They're harmless. No, that's the one beast I won't shoot. I couldn't do it."

"Too bloody true you couldn't do it," he shouted in the isolation of the driving seat. He knew people were not really convinced. "It's that Pratt thing, you know—" he knew they said that. "His friend was killed and he saw it. Don't know exactly what happened, probably the usual thing, thick bush and so on, next thing there you are, up in the air, and dead. Gilligan? Bull got away apparently." But one never knew what people really said about one, did one, he thought. Only what was passed on after being censored in a kindly way. But one thing no one could say was that he was scared of a wild beast. He had fought that battle all the time, smashing them down, lion and buffalo and rhino, standing still till all was ready, and then he let them have it in the right place and down they went. But he could not do it with elephant. He was going to, this time, and that bull had waited up there in that far-gone piece of country, and he was coming to knock it down. "Got to! Got to!" and he was all tense and straining again when he thought of what he wanted to do, and should have done long ago. Sacked the tracker, sent him packing, the only witness who had seen the Bwana legging it, passing him by, going on, all out. Actually passed the African. God! The truck leaped into the air, for in his agonized reverie he had forgotten what he was doing and had let the wheel be torn out of his hands. Brought back to now, and almost spent nervously with what he had gone through once more with his mind, he wrenched the heavy truck back onto the path.

It was nearly dusk. He was tired. He was depressed and remorseful. It might not have been so bad had it just been one of those talkative, boasting bastards like the usual run of the human race, but that it was Pratt he had let down, and had not avenged, had become like some ironic punishment, for Pratt was the only fellow he had ever felt real affection for.

"Here'll do." He steered the truck into a sandy glade under tall mimosas. He braked it to a standstill, and then bent his head until it was heavy on his arms across the steering wheel. He always wished he were dead after these bouts.

11

It was on the fifth day that they came to the Janali Ganjo River, the wide, thickly forested, red-brown river, where the people who had voted against the desert lived. There were two kinds of men; those who loved the desert, and the thirst behind the scrawny camels, and the hysterical fights at water holes after days of semimadness in the sun, and other men, the conquered ones, smaller and blacker and laughing, who had stayed on the river where they had been driven after the conquest. These were the original owners of the great endless country into which the fierce nomads had come generations ago with their long, shining needlelike spears, the gangling spurners of poisoned arrows and the sneaking trap set in the grass, men who liked to slay and chant about it afterward. Now the wilderness belonged to the tall, beautiful, lazy killers, and the long fruitful river belonged, by permission, to the

73

small, chunky, cunning tribes who had forgotten they had once owned the wilderness as well.

Muller could hear their drums throbbing as he stopped his truck. He sat quite still, in that mysterious atavistic excitement which comes when these drums are heard for the first time, the deep rhythmic throbbing which could belong nowhere so rightfully as here among the dark, glossy, luscious leaves and the murmuring glittering brown water with the lianas trailing in it like eels hanging from the trees. He lit a cigarette and then sat, rapt and stirred as the long drums of the Balai sounded out over the savannas along the river. Some had wooden sounds, others sounded like slapped leather, some boomed and rolled, but all were one in a perfect subtle hammering of many tempos. The sun was flashing like gold coins spinning in the racing brown water. A little boy, black and smelling of musk, his big white teeth almost dripping with the juice of his spittle, came up to Muller with a basketful of green limes, mangoes pink and gold, and fat dark bluish melons. Excited and happy, Muller gave him coins and took the basket, rammed his nose into it and breathed up Africa into his nostrils in a long, sharp, acrid freshness, the fruit cold and refreshing against his hot, sweating face. He was done for and he knew it, captured, and would fret forever while away from this place he had discovered. He could see Gilligan standing among a crowd of the small black people in the village beside the water. There was cool dark shade spilled across the sheets of golden glare on the red earth, and bright birds were flicking and darting among the green leaves overhead. After the days of hostile wilderness the village by the river was like the bright smile of the little boy who was looking up at him and learning all the lines and colors of his strange face.

Very happy, wanting to discuss this feeling he had with Gilligan, who seemed to love Africa so much that he owned it, Muller got out of the truck and walked down the hard sun-baked path to the village. He found that Gilligan was questioning the owner of a trade truck about whether he would be willing to take a passenger. The trade-truck driver, a fat, black Arabized man in a turban, was airing his fluent English, and Muller listened for a time and then asked Gilligan who was the passenger. He knew well, but had hoped that time would have resigned Gilligan to Jama's watchful and careful presence in the camp. But no.

"Who? Jama. Who else? It's all fixed. You relax and leave this to me." They were always telling each other now to relax. Muller laughed exasperatedly and said, "Will you cut it out? You ought to join the Mafia, pal. Cut it out, will you, and let the poor guy alone." And then, a fatal move, he turned to the trade-truck owner and said, "You can fade, Joe. Thanks all the same. It was all a horrible mistake. O.K.? Forget it." The trader looked at them both and began to turn away, but Gilligan caught him by the arm and then turned to Muller.

In an undertone he said, "We don't have scenes in this country in front of the *watu*. For Christ's sake will you remember once in a while that you have a white skin, like I have? Now go and have a drink while I fix up about getting rid of Jama. Because he's not staying. I thought of your tender feelings and democracy and Uncle Tom's Cabin and everything, because you couldn't stand seeing a Bushman left where he belongs. So I let him come as far as this, and I told him this was the end. See? Now just don't interfere any more with my affairs, will you?" He grew heated, forgetting the undertone, the watching, puzzled trader, the gathering Africans. "Just mind your own bloody business and leave me to mine."

"Get this into your thick head, pal," Muller snapped back at him. "Jama's mine. I've taken him on. I like him. I get on with him. I'm keeping him. Keeping him. Now do you hear what I said? I *want* him with me. So stop being a jerk and leave it there, will you?"

They were both physically tired after the long wearing day across the hot rocks and sand, and they had been bickering about many things during their halts. Gilligan had never met anyone so formidable and determined as Muller. The fellow looked on everything that happened as a personal challenge and had become unbearable. He had some kind of complex about being American, or about not knowing the country; whatever it was it had become a bloody nuisance, and he had had enough of it.

Jama was sitting down smoking a cigarette under a tree nearby, watching with interest while the two men had their quarrel about him. He wanted to see Gilligan lose, though he admired him, and hated him too. He wanted to see the American bend Gilligan's will. He was almost laughing at the expression of outrage on Gilligan's face as he listened to Muller, and then he watched Muller when Gilligan spoke. There was something ridiculous about the way the two white men, who had been arguing and picking at each other every day, were now telling the trader to go, and then to stay, one pushing him away and the other pulling him back.

"O.K.," Muller said, shrugging his shoulders. "Fix it

all up if you like, but Jama's staying. You interfere any more with my servants and by Christ you'll get trouble. I mean it, Gilligan. Nothing would give me greater pleasure than to have a workout with you if that's what you want. Is it what you want?"

"A workout?"

"A workout. A fight. Is that what you're after?"

"Now listen, Muller. Don't be silly now. I could kill you with one hand if I wanted, and you know it. Will you be sensible, please, and go and have a drink, and let me run my safari? I've done my best to have no trouble with you for the last three days, hard though it's been. You don't like me, I know. Fine. O.K. You're entitled to your opinions. But you're not entitled to bugger my staff about and to flout my orders. No one does it, do you understand? No one.

"The crowd's getting bigger. Don't forget we're two white men together in darkest Africa. What will the natives think? We mustn't behave like this in front of the natives." Muller was laughing with rage as he spoke. He turned away and saw Jama. He called him. He gave him a handful of shillings. "Go and buy me some pineapples. I saw a woman carrying pineapples." He winked at Jama. "Keep out of the way until we pull out of here." He watched Jama move away through the crowd into the heart of the village. Gilligan did not know what to do next. So he laughed bitterly and made his way out of the crowd, to find time to try and think.

12

JAMA HAD NOW BECOME A "THING," a problem of greater importance than his service, between Muller and Gilligan. Muller saw this as he idled about among the stalls in the hot village, sullen and resentful. He tried to see the business for what it was, something to do with justice and humanity, and, most of all—he smiled wryly as he faced it— a symbol of who was going to win, who could master the other, between two personalities which should separate as soon as possible. They were too like each other, Muller knew that. 'But at least I'm more reasonable, more willing to play ball,' Muller agreed with himself. 'At least I *know* what's going on here. I do know all this is crazy but with a guy like Gilligan no one can ever afford to back down. I've never met a guy I wanted more to get the better of. He just *makes* me want to win.' And he hated Gilligan for that easy ability. He was responding to Gilligan readily, and he saw clearly how he was doing it.

It might have been different if, on that first morning
when he had arrived and met Gilligan for the first time,
he had said brightly, "Sure. O.K. You want to move right
now? Fine. Let's go." But he never let anyone do that
kind of thing to him and he had known at once that
Gilligan was trying him out, and he had stayed Muller,
had his way, and Gilligan, probably in a raging temper,
had sacked Jama, and the thing was on.

He bought a pair of camel-hide sandals and a finely
made skinning knife in a rawhide sheath. He drank the
cold milk from green coconuts, ate some tiny fragrant
bananas, followed, as he sauntered in the thick sand of
the street, by a string of silent small boys who watched
everything he did. The drums throbbed all the time and
he quietly and unobtrusively eyed the women who
watched him, grinning, as his light eyes flickered on their
glistening blackness. All this fresh, green riot of plant and
tree about him splashed with deep dark shadow, and the
black people without tension in them, and the sense of
something that he felt could not last very long, put him
into a mood of friendly melancholy, so that he thought
he loved everybody he saw here, from old withered men
to small naked boys who somersaulted in the hot sand
and then looked at him with big, staring expectant eyes,
grinning. He thought he knew why Gilligan hated civilization so much and why he gave the impression of a man
who thought he was the protector of all this innocent
unawareness of the advance of the cement mixers and the
soul engineers. He was in such a puzzling state of light-
hearted, good-natured melancholy when he thought of
their stupid hostility to each other that he was ready to
seek Gilligan out and say, "Look, pal, I've been a goddam

fool. You're right. You run this safari your way. Sack
Jama. From here on I'm just a passenger." But he was not
going to do it, because Gilligan was a mean bastard who
needed stopping, needed to be shown where to get off.
"I've never let anyone push me around and I can't start
now. I'm right and I'm going to stay right, and the
bastard knows I'm right too. He's suffering with it, and
that's right too."

He stopped to watch some youths shooting arrows
through a sapling which they had bound into a circle and
had hung from an overhanging bough. Their bows were
long and polished, of some attractive blackish wood,
and the arrowheads were slivers of shining metal fitted
into long yellow durable reeds. One of the youths offered
him his bow and the others gathered about him and gave
advice about how to use the first two fingers of the right
hand for gripping the flight of the arrow and pulling on
the string. After a few shots he sent one through the
circle and the Africans all jumped up and down, stiff
legged, and yelled as if they had just come into money.
The gut bowstring took some pulling, but he drew it as
far as it would go, vain as they clicked their tongues and
nodded admiringly at him. His fingers were raw when he
had finished, and the inside of his left wrist was bruised
from the slap of the bowstrings against it. He wanted to
buy one of the bows and a quiver of arrows but they
refused, solemnly, and he liked them for that, though
annoyed.

He went back to the trucks about sunset and had some
tea which Aganaza made for him. Aganaza said Bwana
Gilligan was still in the village. "He have friend here,"
Aganaza said in eager English, a language Gilligan would

never allow him to use in his presence. "Drink with Indian trader." He lifted an invisible glass to his lips, one in each hand, adding, "Sell skins here in old times. Many friend here for Bwana." While Aganaza was talking Muller was listening to a powerful clear voice singing "Roses of Picardy" and coming nearer until it was in the camp, and then he saw Gilligan, supported by two Africans, being led toward him. He was pretty drunk, but not too drunk to sit down carefully opposite Muller, lean his chin on his hands, gaze into Muller's eyes, and say, "You're getting on my nerves, chum. Do you know that? You're getting me down. What's your next plan? What's the bloody game exactly?"

"Smoke?" Muller proffered a tin of cigarettes, taking his time before replying, knowing it would be useless, and embarrassing too, to treat Gilligan like a drunken man, say to him, "Now look, you're boozed, pal. Let's leave it till tomorrow." Gilligan took a cigarette from the tin without fumbling, unfalteringly, and Muller lit it for him.

"Well?" Gilligan spoke through smoke, as if now in full control of himself. "*Leta* whisky," he shouted loudly without turning his head. "*Na belauri mbili, na* soda. *Upesi*," and, ready for this, Aganaza came on like an actor, with a tray holding a bottle of whisky, glasses, and bottles of soda.

"I want to know *why* you're fighting me," Gilligan said while he poured whisky into two glasses. He poured big drinks for both of them, handed one to Muller. "You're getting on my wick, chum," he said. "And I'm not putting up with much more of it."

"You're sick, Gilligan," Muller said in a knowing and

yet friendly way. "Sick. Why? You're adequate. Why this aggressiveness all the time? What's eating you? It's not me. It's everything. Why pick on me? You know you're wasting your time. Quit pushing. I'm tired of it."

"Sick? Who's sick? Me? Here, give my your hand and let's see who's sick." Gilligan leaned his right elbow on the table and held out his hooked right hand for Muller to grasp, ready for Indian wrestling. He was smiling, hardly able to wait to press Muller's arm down on the table. Muller knew all this as soon as he saw that big hooked hand come out to take his. He had done this himself many a time.

"I don't mean that kind of sick," he said. "I mean the other kind of sick. You're carrying a big load, pal, and you want to drop it on everybody. What's it about? Why this aggression? Why do you want to get on top of me? What good will it do you, even if you *could* get on top? I'm a big boy now. I'm past this stuff—"

"Get hold of my bloody hand," Gilligan said impatiently, like a man who has heard enough excuses and put up with enough prevarication. "Too much talk, chum. Let's see what you can *do*. That's the test. What a fellow can actually *do*. Right?"

"I don't want to *do* anything. I want to find out what the hell is eating you, that's all. This is kid stuff. But what are the facts? I won't let you have some revenge on Jama? I'm tired of this goddam stuff. I'm going to bed."

"Get hold of that hand," Gilligan ordered him. "Go on. Get hold of it and let's see what you can do. I'm sick of your bloody boasting, chum. That's all you do, is say what you can do. But what *can* you do? Get hold of it."

Muller's hesitation had made him heady and had greatly increased his determination, and he wanted to punish Muller and make him respectful. But Muller was still not done with the talk. Gilligan, still holding out his hand, listened to him with an ironical smile on his thin mouth.

"You need to talk to somebody," Muller was saying. "You're a guy who could be liked. Don't kid me that you're one of these people who don't care if they're not liked. You're sick and you know why, too. Why don't you face it? A thing's nothing once you face it."

"Are you making hints about something?" Gilligan's eyes had kindled and, as if regretful for what he had said, twitched his hand and said, "Come on. Let's see what you can *do*."

"You're boozed, pal. I don't want to do any calisthenics with you while you're boozed. Tomorrow."

"No, now. Now." Gilligan jerked his head and twitched his hand. "Don't fool yourself, I'm not boozed."

"O.K. I'll hold you then. You won't move my hand. No one can do that. So don't start screaming if you can't move my hand." Muller took his hand. They leveled their elbows until they were exactly opposite each other.

"You're allowed to grip the table with your left hand, but no pushing. Just operate from the shoulder—"

"*I* know the goddam rules," Muller said angrily. He wanted to defeat and humiliate Gilligan now.

"Right," Gilligan said. "You ready?"

"I've been ready for days."

"I know you have. And now you can show me what you can do."

They put the pressure on and the struggle began. About twenty yards away, sitting on a chop-box, a cigar-

ette forgotten in his hand, Aganaza watched. He had
seen the Bwana on so many occasions getting the better
of his friends. The Bwana, a good but difficult man, had
never been beaten, but he did not seem to be able to press
the other Bwana's hand back, and the other Bwana seemed
under no strain. He stood up and watched more closely,
taking a few paces forward in his absorption, fearful for
Bwana Gilligan, who was so strong that most men's arms
were pressed down in a few seconds by him.

Gilligan had never come up against an arm as strong as
this one now holding him with apparent ease. Muller was
still and tense, his eyes steady, and watched Gilligan's
face while the great force they had summoned met in
their hands. Gilligan was absorbed in what he was trying
to do, too absorbed, with that almost desperate attention
of a man who is getting an unexpected surprise where
none was anticipated. He put on more and more pressure,
glancing at Muller and smiling fiercely. A film of sweat
had come out on his forehead, but he was still confident
that all would be well. Muller could not keep this up.
No one could keep this up against what he, Gilligan, could
turn on. But the shock he had been given had begun to
drip down into his will and doubt was on him. He could
not move Muller's hand back even half an inch. Muller's
hand held him there. It was like pushing against a stone
wall. Worse, Muller was smoking with his left hand,
not even gripping the table, and Gilligan knew he was
doing it to show how unperturbed he was. This insulting
gesture almost caused him to lose his head. It was seeing
Jama walk up to watch which demoralized Gilligan. He
put everything he had into his massive right arm, so much

that he began to quiver. His face darkened to a brick color, but Muller held him.

"Say when," Muller said calmly. Gilligan flashed a look of hatred at him and a pearl of sweat rolled down into his eye. He kept up the pressure for nearly another minute and still Muller's hand did not move. He wanted a rest but he could not make himself give up. This had never happened to him before and a sort of hysteria was coming over him. He fell back on diplomacy, and, still pressing against Muller's immovable hand, said, "You want a rest?"

"*You* want the rest, pal. Not me," Muller said, smiling at him. And it was true. Gilligan could not keep it up. He relaxed his push, ungripped his hand from Muller's, breathing very audibly, saw Jama and stood up, shouting, "Get to hell out of this camp or I'll kill you." He seemed as if he might go berserk. Jama smiled at him insolently and strolled slowly away toward the camp fire. Gilligan stood there, grief-haunted, and Muller, sorry for him, while enjoying that terrible male feeling of victory, said, "Come on, Gill, sit down. Jeeze, you've got some power in that right arm there."

"Don't you patronize me," Gilligan said harshly. "I won't take it. That was round one. You didn't move me, you know. You can't. It was a draw."

Muller shook his head in compassionate denial of this, saying, "I didn't try, Gill. You want me to try?"

"Pour me another drink." Gilligan was touched by being called Gill by this enemy, but he would not let it soften his resolve. This fellow was set upon humiliating him, God alone knew why. Touchiness? Look at the ready way he had done that business on the first morning, fighting, aggressive, where it had been quite unnecessary. He could not keep the hatred out of his eyes as he looked at Muller pouring out two more whiskies.

At the next contest Gilligan felt the pressure come on immediately, and he held it, shaking, for about twenty seconds, and then, a fraction at a time, began to yield. And Muller, all male again, his compassion gone, had his teeth bared until he flattened Gilligan's arm on the table.

"There you are, pal," Muller said, his voice deep after the struggle. "Want to try the left hand now? Let's really knock ourselves out."

Gilligan was good in defeat. His face had turned pale and seemed to have become drawn, hollow. Muller was watching him intensely, as if he expected Gilligan to spring at him.

"I'm a bit boozed, that's what it is," Gilligan told him, swallowing with some effort. He was almost nervously out of control after the strain, and the grievous shock he had received. Muller knew everything he was feeling, was sorry for him, and glad to have defeated him. Everything had changed. Everything.

"How old are you?" Gilligan asked Muller.

"Forty."

"And you were in the war?"

"Yeah. Who wasn't?"

"Kill anybody? I mean personally. I don't mean this bloody nonsense of firing artillery or dropping bombs. I mean action. Did you kill anybody in the war?" Gilligan was staring into his eyes as if expecting lies and ready to see them and accuse them.

"Forty-six Japs." Muller could not keep the self-satisfaction out of his voice, and Gilligan stared at him, quite unashamedly testing his own doubts by looking ironically into Muller's amused eyes.

"Too many Japs?" Muller asked. "Want me to trim it down, maybe?" He laughed, while Gilligan watched his eyes. He knew he and Gilligan were two of those men who never got over their wars, never could taste life with the same savor again as they had tasted it in war. These men spent a lot of time together, like this, examining each other's credentials, giving and taking away respect, but glad to give it if it was deserved. He and Gilligan had not questioned each other up to now, not established any intimacy greater than the anxiety and hatred they had caused in each other. "How about you?" Muller went on.

"You mean was *I* in the war?" Gilligan cocked his eyebrows and dilated his nostrils. "You asked me that in one of your letters. Remember? Was *I* in the war?" He laughed with anger. "*Was I in the war?* Forty-six Japs, eh? Or was it twenty-three, with mortar bombs or hand grenades?" Seeing Muller's ready anger he went on, "You're telling me, sitting right here, that you killed forty-six Japs personally. Right?"

"That's what I'm telling you. And don't you start any of this superman stuff about it. I'm not taking it. It's a wonder some guy hasn't strangled you before now, do you know that? You're a bad-mannered, difficult bastard to deal with, but don't you try and kick my war record around, because I'm proud of it, and the sooner I see the back of you the better I'll like it."

"Same here," Gilligan replied, narrowing his eyes as he spoke, so melodramatically that Muller laughed despite his rage. "Now you say you shot those Japs. With a rifle or a machine gun? I'm merely asking as a technician. I've killed more men than you have, Muller, and the matter interests me—"

"You've killed more than I have? When? Where?"

"I was in *two* wars, chum. Two. The last war was nothing. A picnic compared with the Somme and Ypres. Ten million bloody shells before the attack, chum. That was World War I. There was nothing like that in the last war and you know it. So don't come around here shouting the bloody odds about what you did in the last war. The last war was nothing." He got to his feet, worked up. "Nothing, chum. I have a respect for the experienced soldier, no matter what race he belongs to. But I don't like boasting and shouting the bloody odds."

Gilligan hammered the camp table with his fist. Muller's face was tight and pale, his hands gripping the side of the table while Gilligan's ranting voice went on. "Then you make hints. *Hints.* Why not come out in the open with what you meant to say? Someone's been talking about me in Nairobi or Mombasa and you lap it up and then make hints. What was it this time? My social habits? Or about Pratt?" He brought his fist down on the table, an expression of vicious cunning suddenly coming into his eyes. "Pratt's death was all in the game, chum, and that's all about it."

"You're loaded," Muller said. "You're boozed up. Let's break this up. Let's call this goddam safari off. You go back to Guyu and leave Chongu with me. I'll get the elephant. I think it would be a good thing if you and me separated right now." He held up his hand. "Don't say

anything more about the war. I can't take any more of
it. Now quit the war talk. You're boozed." 'He's mad.
Remember he's mad. He's not responsible,' he kept
telling himself. There was a strange look in Gilligan's
eyes, like that in the eyes of a man seeing a vision.

"You've been set on making trouble ever since you got
to my camp by the Waso Larok River," Gilligan said.
"I knew it the moment I opened my mouth. You thought
I was trying to stop you having your breakfast—"

"And weren't you?" Muller shouted, exasperated.

"Only for a good reason." Gilligan leaned forward and
put his face so close to Muller's that Muller could smell
the warm healthy scent of his skin, could look into the
mad blue eyes and see tiny yellow flecks around the
small black pupils. There was something magnificent about
Gilligan's twisted and aggressive personality which both
impressed and amused him. "You think I don't know what
they say about me?" Gilligan said. "You think I don't
know they make out I'm a bush stiff, mad, dangerous,
argumentative, and the rest of it? What do I care what
these bloody little ants among their buildings and in their
clubs think about me? I'm a proud man, chum." He sat
up proudly, laying his hand on his chest. "Things are
going wrong in this camp. And they've gone wrong since
you interfered and picked up that Somali and started to
spoil him. I've taken him on my staff again and you're
not to speak to him again. You're to have nothing to do
with him. Nothing. Do you hear? Nothing." Gilligan
was pressing his fists on the table and quivering with the
force of his worked-up emotions.

"You've taken him on again?" Muller looked be-
wildered. "You mean he's working for you again?"

"That's what I mean. And from now on I run this camp and everything in it."

"Where's Jama?" Muller was wounded, was already deeply involved in that mysterious sense of possession about Africa, about loyalty and being liked and knowing what was right and good for the natives. He was hurt to think that Jama could have agreed to desert him, for he had formed a possessive affection for the intelligent Somali he had saved from the desert.

"There he is," Gilligan pointed dramatically at Jama, who was moving about uneasily as if haunted by some guilt, about twenty yards away, his eyes on the two white men.

"Jama, come over here," Muller shouted. He was staring accusingly at the Somali, who would not meet his eyes properly. Jama came over with his eyes fixed on Gilligan. Gilligan said, *"Mwambia Bwana shauri ile sisi na tanganeza ndani ya mji leo."*

Jama, now that he was cornered, put a hard face on it and turned to look at Muller with unflinching eyes, Muller who was gazing angrily and pleadingly into his eyes for some word which would assure him that his trust and friendship had not been betrayed.

"I work for Bwana Gilligan now," Jama said. "Bwana say he not angry with me no more. All right now. He say—"

"How much did he give you? What was your price?" Muller asked bitterly. "I want to know the goddam score, that's all. What goes on?"

"Kwenda!" Gilligan said to Jama. "You can go." As Jama went gladly and swiftly away, Gilligan rose to his feet, shouting in Ki-Swahili, a note of iron command in

his voice which carried across the camp. As always when in a state of emotion, and addressing the Africans, he mixed English slang and curses into his Ki-Swahili. "Now get this bloody *kampi fungaed* up *upesi* because we're bloody *kwendaing sasa hivi, na sakiyo? Na* bloody *sakiyo mimi? Funga vyombo* bloody *yoti na tanganeza vitu yoti tayari mara moja sababu sisi na piga safari sasa. Upesi. Na sakiyo?* Bloody *upesi.*"

When he saw the Africans hurrying about in the fire-light as Gilligan shouted, Africans picking up kits and running to the trucks, Muller said, "What's going on now?"

"Going on?" said Gilligan. "Nothing extraordinary. We're moving, that's all. We cover the rest of the safari tonight. Tomorrow we walk, after your elephant."

"Now listen—" Muller began.

"Listen nothing," Gilligan shouted. "I know what I'm doing. We're going and that's all about it. This is my safari, an illegal one, I might add, and I'm running it. Now go and see to your kit. There are game scouts not far from here this side of the river and I want to move, that's all. Now will you be a big boy and do what I say?"

They looked at each other for half a minute, completely incensed with each other, Muller saying in a low voice, "I'll never forget you. Never. If ever I wanted to put my hands round a guy's—" but Gilligan had left him, shouting orders to the Africans. This was his psychological warfare. There were no game scouts. There was no need to move camp just now, but he wanted to break Muller's growing influence in the camp, his easy way with the Africans, and have command all the time. He had waylaid Jama in the market of the village and had done something he had never done in his life before, to any-body, black or white. He had apologized and had offered his hand to Jama, who had immediately seized it in an emotional and almost tearful gladness, for no white man had ever apologized to him before. He did not like Gil-ligan but he respected him, yet it was the unexpected gesture from Gilligan which had overcome his stubborn resentment for the way he had been treated by him.

"I'll increase your pay by ten shillings a month," Gil-ligan said. "And I'm sorry for what I did, providing you're sorry for drawing that knife on me." He showed nothing of the great suffering he was enduring in this abasing of himself to win back Jama. He looked his old self, steady, confident, stern, yet tender in this amazing moment.

"I work for you again," Jama said.

"Bwana," Gilligan reminded him, putting a foot forward again into his old area of command, out of the nauseating area of apology he had forced himself to enter after hours of agonizing appraisal.

"Bwana," Jama said, recovered now from his emotion, glad of what he had done, but grabbing back his dignity as fast as he could. "You no shout me, Bwana, I no do bad things." He wanted Gilligan to treat him with more respect than he treated the other Africans, the flat-nosed slave people who had no dignity. Gilligan hid the spurt of anger which Jama's effort to bargain with him had aroused.

"You do good work," he said. "And we will have no more trouble," and thought, looking into Jama's eyes, 'You hard-faced bastard. When this safari's over I'll kick your arse so hard for you you won't be able to walk.'

The two trucks crossed the pontoon bridge across the

river in bright moonlight, Muller at the wheel of his truck, aggrieved, embittered, and worried by the hatred he was feeling for Gilligan. He felt it was all going to end in a fight, in which he would half kill the big boorish, crazy man who had not been able to conceal the zest he was feeling in his victory about Jama.

'I mean why didn't I go back after one look at this guy?' Muller was thinking. 'Why didn't I go back?'

It was still dark, about five o'clock in the morning, when Gilligan stopped his truck and got out to greet Muller as the other truck stopped beside him.

Gilligan was friendly, almost flippant, smiling up at Muller as he said, "Well Muller, feel hungry? A nice breakfast and a couple of hours' sleep, eh? This is as far as we can go by truck. Shank's mare after this." He was feeling happy and confident, and he spoke to the sulking, grim American as if nothing had ever marred their relationship. Muller, amazed, watched him and shook his head to show that he could not understand this switch of mood. Gilligan did not take any hint from this, but leaned on the truck door and offered Muller a cigarette. 'He's got his way and now everything's jake,' Muller thought irritably. 'And I'm to be pleasant.'

"You're a fantastic guy, Gilligan," he said.

"It's Gilligan now, is it? It was Gill back in the camp. Don't tell me you're still brooding about this bloody Somali." Gilligan's voice was still pleasant, almost breezy. He was smiling.

"Forget it. Breakfast's a good idea."

"There's game galore here. We'll shoot some meat after we've had a sleep," Gilligan suggested. "I want to see what you can do with a rifle."

13

It was muller's shooting which changed Gilligan's friendly mood to one of jealousy and resentment. He stood far back in incredulous silence and watched Muller shoot down a running oryx with a brain shot, at about three hundred yards, reload almost imperceptibly at the shoulder—one swift flick of the bolt—and then he knocked another one down, another brain shot. The two big beasts fell as if hit by lightning. He could hardly believe what he had seen.

"Think that'll be enough meat, Gilligan?" Muller shouted, without turning around, still watching the moving herd trailing its long ribbons of red dust. "Shall I knock another one off?"

"Yes. Knock another one down," Gilligan said. "We've got the boys to eat them," and Muller brought the rifle up into his shoulder. The game was about four hundred yards away by now. There was the flat explosion and the short, sharp shriek of the .318 Express bullet and another oryx fell. It was extraordinary shooting, so casual, better than Gilligan had ever seen, better than anything he had ever done himself. He stood there, morose and stunned. He felt as if Muller had saved all this up in secret, never hinting about what he could do, and had now as good as said, "Let's see you beat that, pal."

Muller came back to where Gilligan was standing with his hands on his hips. The way Gilligan said nothing, made no remark on the shooting, gave no praise at all, was enormous, like a cloud, and Muller looked at him, smiling, friendly, sardonic. Muller, knowing Gilligan as he did now, knew what Gilligan was feeling. He heard the anger in Gilligan's voice when he called the Africans to the trucks. He could see the grim look on Gilligan's face as they got into the trucks and drove across the gray, paperlike grass toward the dead oryx. 'He's really burned up,' Muller thought with satisfaction. 'If ever I saw a guy going through it, a vain big-headed bastard eating crow, it's Mister Gilligan right now. We'll finish up by doing push-ups in the bush, I know it, and he'll die doing more push-ups than me." It was studying Gilligan that had caused him to see for the first time in his life, with wonder, what he himself was like, what all men who had to be testing themselves all the time were going through. And what was it all for? What was at the bottom of it? Fear? Was fear actually bravery but jacked up by continual training and drive? Flashes of spiteful temper revealed Gilligan's new mood, the way he shouted at Aganaza and the two skinners when giving orders about the three dead oryx. Muller watched him, smiling and yet full of pity, for the strange thing about Gilligan was the way Muller felt he ought not to do anything very well, so as to keep poor Gilligan happy. And this feeling was enough to demolish his pity. Gilligan was unreasonable without needing to say anything. He had that kind of personality which projected itself all the time, a massive, tender vanity which was a menace.

"D'you think I'll do?" Muller asked him, provoked by Gilligan's pointed silence, and by his surly glances.

"You want me to praise your shooting? Is that it?"

"Sure. It's good shooting." Muller had been thrown off balance by Gilligan's question. "Better damn shooting than you've ever seen before. You're killing yourself trying not to say so. Admit it." He had lost his temper again. He began to show it, raising his voice, ashamed of what he had said—and he had only said what he believed—and trying to fortify it.

Gilligan looked at him, soothed and comforted, and appearing amusedly disgusted.

"You were shaken, pal," Muller went on. "Shaken. And why not? You've been preaching all about the open-air life and the world of the great pioneers like yourself, and all about how you can lick anybody at anything. And I shook you with my little rifle just now. But you were dying trying not to show it. Why don't you open up and live? What's wrong with admitting you've had a surprise? And boy, you've had a surprise, haven't you?"

"What's all this *about*?" Gilligan asked him with maddening innocence. "What am I to do? Stand on my bloody hands or something? What the hell's the matter with you?"

"I think you and me need treatment," Muller shouted,

deeply ashamed of himself, but infuriated too. "People like you and me shouldn't be allowed to meet."

"Speak for yourself," Gilligan told him. "We'll move off in a couple of hours, when you're ready."

14

AFTER THE FIRST TWO HOURS on foot Muller began to feel the heat, began to wonder if they could not march at night, when it would be cool. It was some years since he had carried a rifle on the march in this kind of sun and it weighed heavily on its shoulder sling. He would not have felt so apprehensive had it not been for the continual and compulsive competition between himself and Gilligan.

They walked beside each other, the Africans spread out behind with their loads. The country was all ravines and rocks here and ahead were mountains on which green-blue forest glistened like glossy hair in the almost blinding sun glare. The sun felt like hot acid on Muller's skin. Sweat was rolling down his face. He had never walked under a sun like this one. He began to worry about water, a shadow of fear of thirst crossing his mind, but

Gilligan would know all about that. It was not possible to say casually to Gilligan, "Will we be all right for water?" It was too risky to ask such a question, for Gilligan would see fear in it.

"Feeling O.K.?" Gilligan asked.

"*I'm* O.K.," Muller replied, too swiftly, too much accent on the "I'm," he knew. 'Watch it. You're going as crazy as this guy if you don't look out.' "Sure, I'm feeling fine. You?"

"Listen. You can tell *me* what they said to you about me back in Nairobi, Muller. I know, as a matter of fact, but I just want it confirmed. It was about Pratt, wasn't it?" Gilligan was deceptively careless in the way he spoke, no sign of his real urgency in his tone.

"About Pratt? What *is* this Pratt business, Gilligan? What the hell is eating you about it?" 'He wants to unload,' Muller thought. 'A version anyway.'

"Why Gilligan? Why not Gill? Are you still nursing some grudge or other about the bastard behind us?" Jama was carrying the .500 and the ammunition about ten yards behind them.

"O.K. O.K., Gill. Now, about Pratt. You've got some kind of thing about this guy, Pratt. Want to tell me about it?"

"Pratt, as a matter of fact, was the only fellow I've ever liked in my whole life. I mean *liked*."

"So he died."

"That's right. So he died. Because I liked him, probably, he died. That's the way with everything. You like it and it lets you down—"

"You mean Pratt died on you deliberately?"

"More or less. No, bugger you, I don't mean that at all, and you know it. Why are you always doing this kind of thing, Muller? Does it give you pleasure to upset me? Well, no matter. Pratt. No, I mean he was the best friend I ever had and he was killed. It seems queer to me, that. I never made another friend before or since."

"What about Graig?"

"A parasite. A weakling attached to a strong person. That's all that is. Graig's a bush stiff, a bum. No harm in him. No, I'm talking about friendship. Friendship for me means *I* will do anything for my friend. I never felt that about anyone except Pratt. And yet he wasn't like me at all."

'I'll bet he wasn't. It would be impossible, Joe, to find anyone like you.' "And he was killed. What happened?"

"The elephant picked him up and bashed him against a rock and killed him. That's what happened. Now tell me the *dirty* story, the one people prefer, the one they invented and tell about me. How I let Pratt down and so on. Go on. I'm listening. I don't care, you know. I know all this stuff. But I'd like to hear if the story's the same or if it's been embellished."

"Listen, Gill. I want you to believe this and not to argue with me about it. I've heard *no* story about you and Pratt. Get it? Are you listening to me? I've heard no story about you and Pratt. No story. Nothing. So what happened?"

Gilligan did not reply. They walked on over the hot sand, Muller's rubber soles squeaking slightly on the scattered shale. Muller waited.

"I don't particularly want to discuss it," Gilligan said.

"He was my friend and I saw him killed. But I know these stories have gone about. People are petty little bastards, you know, and they prefer disaster to the facts. I've no time for bloody people. None."

"I've gathered that."

"Why? Do you like them yourself?"

"They don't worry me as much as they worry you. I just let them get on with living, and I get on with living. I never cared a damn what anyone thought about me."

"There you go again, you see, Muller. You're a queer chap, you know. You could be a likable bloke if it weren't for your chip on the shoulder. What's that chip *about*?"

"*My* chip? Are you crazy? *My* chip?" Muller laughed.

"Oh, you have a chip all right. And a big one. You remind me of what I was like when I was your age, a few years ago, always on the watch for things. Trying to outdo the other fellow all the time. You know what that is? Doubt. Worry. What is it that worries you all the time? What are you trying to prove to yourself?"

"You're not kidding me, are you?" Muller could hardly speak for laughter, hearing Gilligan describe himself in this way. "*My* chip? Well, to get back to Pratt, then. What happened?"

"I told you. He was killed. And now we're going after the elephant that killed him. That's all."

"And you've never been this way since?"

"Never been this way since. It's a long way to come, as you've noticed. I don't want the elephant. You want it. So I'm taking you after it. That's it, isn't it?"

"But you don't want to come after it yourself? Did

you get a thing about this elephant after it killed your friend? I'd have got a thing about that. Yes, I'd have got a thing about an elephant after that."

"What you'd get and what I'd get would be different things," said Gilligan. "I don't get a thing about anything, you see? It's a big elephant and it's got brains. And it lives well away from everybody. I have no thing about it. I'm down here because you want the elephant and I want the money. That's why I'm here. I have no thing. Elephants don't interest me. Show me a lion or a buff or a rhino and I'm your man. I'll flatten them before you say knife. But I've nothing against elephants. If I was an animal I'd like to be an elephant. I've nothing against them. They harm no one if they're left alone. Elephants are all right. And if it weren't for the money I wouldn't be here taking you after this elephant."

"You missed it after it killed Pratt? What happened?"

"Missed it?"

"You shot at it, surely? What happened? Or don't you want to talk about it?"

"What makes you think I don't want to talk about it? What are you getting at? Are you trying to get at something? What's on your mind? You can tell me, you know. Somebody's been telling you stories. What's it all about?" There was no anger or anxiety in Gilligan's voice.

"*You* said you didn't want to talk about it, pal. Not me. Right? But why don't you want to talk about it? So you didn't shoot at it. It killed Pratt and that was it."

"Thick bush, forest. It got away. It's tough country. You'll be in it tomorrow and you'll see."

Muller stole a look at Gilligan and saw his eyes staring ahead, fixed, haunted, his mouth sad, right off guard.

"I won't talk about it any more," Muller said.

"You've got it into your head that I've got a thing about this bloody elephant," Gilligan said sharply. "Get it out of your mind. Stop harping on the bloody thing, will you? You're all the same, you Americans, full of this bloody psychology thing and digging about looking for meanings in things. Life's simpler than that. It's life. If you get killed by this elephant when we find it, do you think I'm going to have a thing about it?"

"I won't get killed by any elephant, pal. Don't try and scare me."

"You're impossible to talk to, Muller. It's this bloody chip you have. It's a bore. A bore." They were silent after that, and Muller began to notice the heat again and to feel the weight of his rifle.

15

MULLER COULD NOT bring himself to suggest they have a rest. His mind teemed with sentences, with various forms of casually spoken suggestions, and all were rejected by the devil sitting on top of his mind, the devil he had got to know so well in the war, and which he had let in out of fear, not fear of death but of a man's opinion. He had been a coward in his bravery, on a blasted hill on Okinawa. He had been a captain then, full of honors and reputation, fit and hard and matching his trained and willing blood lust with his ready, waiting fear, that fear so slender that it slips in through a crack while a man is not watching.

They had been standing on a hill after a mind-shaking battle and the hill was covered with Japanese dead, all of them still warm, and the country around them full of the noise of automatic fire as the fighting continued against the willing, dogged enemy troops who were here to die to the last man. The officer standing with Muller was a fellow captain in the same battalion, and like Muller he was dusty, in need of a shave, shaken, exhilarated, spent but still watchful and ready for action. A Nambu ahead of them opened fire and the bursts hissed and cracked in the air on the right of the two captains, and then moved nearer to them. Neither of them moved but stood watching, as if unconcerned, the moving infantry patrol advancing against a Japanese bunker below them. The machine-gun fire came nearer and Muller waited for his companion to lie down, when he would lie down too, but his companion was waiting for Muller to give in first, and Muller did not move. The air just above their heads began to flutter and pulse with rushes of machine-gun bullets, and they still stood, looking cool, each waiting for the other to give in, and Muller gave in first. He threw himself on his face, and two or three seconds later, it must have been at least three seconds Muller reckoned, his companion lay down beside him, slowly and as if casually, but tired of face and smile, worn by his effort to win, and he had smiled at Muller and said, "Jeeze, fella, you went down so fast I thought some bastard had shot you. Feeling O.K.?"

No, you could not afford to let yourself down with these guys, guys like Gilligan and that captain. Every time he thought of that captain's weary, frightened eyes when he had made that dirty remark as they lay side by side under the machine-gun flail, he wished he had killed the bastard right there. It had had an enormous effect on him, that remark, and in a way had forced him to use that incident in Okinawa as a kind of measuring board of how he was doing as a hundred-per-cent man, or rather, Man. That captain had been yellow, and working his yellowness on the brave whom he could not bear to see unafraid. Gilligan was the same, and you should never soften up with them, never try and understand them, or you were through, done for. They wanted to stand over you and crow.

He changed the rifle to the other shoulder and licked his dry lips, certain now that Gilligan was working up a great big contest between them, in silence, walking beside him in apparent comfort under the fierce sun glare, and he had never moved his rifle from his right shoulder. Gilligan's rifle was a .500, far heavier than the rifle Muller was carrying, and for nearly half an hour Muller worked out the differences in weight of the two rifles, their differences of age, fretting and worrying while he slipped the rifle over to the other shoulder, and sure that Gilligan was noticing it all. (Should he get the other .500 from Jama and carry it?)

'I mustn't let my imagination run away with me. I'm behaving like a kid. What the hell's the matter with me?' Everything. 'Surely this guy feels like having a rest? I mean what's a rest? All he has to do is say, "Let's have ten minutes sit down," normal like that, and you sat down and there you were. I mean what goes on? We've been walking in this goddam sun for hours and I'm *certain* he must feel like a rest, and a drink. So he's working another situation up, he's waiting for me to suggest a rest, like that bastard on Okinawa that day, and what happened when I did lie down? The bastard crowed. Are we to go through this kind of thing all our goddam lives? I mean what's it all supposed to be for? He's waiting for me to speak first, and I know he's dying for a rest, but he can wait because I'll walk till I drop before I open my trap. I'll walk this maniac right into the ground.'

It gave him fresh life, this anger, but he was feeling the huge weight of the blazing sun above them, and Gilligan showed no sign of discomfort. 'Don't get steamed up,' Muller counseled himself. 'Keep cool. Cool? Jeeze I feel like I'm being fried. But you had your lesson with those yellow guys that day on Okinawa, and never forget it. He won't speak about what happened with this elephant but if ever I saw a guy suffering it was Gilligan when I was rubbing his wound. Something dirty happened, I know it, and he knows I know it, and that's what's the matter here. He's fighting me like I was some enemy or something. These guys are enough to drive you mad with their problems. They use their problems like weapons. Defense mechanisms, overcompensations and like that. Jesus, but I could drink a river. Take it straight, pal. Be calm. He'll fold first. Let him fold first. That'll be the moment. And that's what he needs, more of that stuff, like when I pressed his goddam hand down on that table, jeeze did he look bad or didn't he? Couldn't speak. That killed him all right, that shock. He's bigger than me, and I'm big, but you have to have what it takes, pal, and I'VE GOT IT, PAL. I'VE GOT IT. I wonder what he's like with women. Yellow, I'll bet. Runs away from them. Can't imagine him with one of them anyway. No, that's true, you can't imagine him with a woman, talking with one and feeling confident and everything; all kind of twisted up into a knot about everything.'

"Did you ever marry?" he asked Gilligan.

"I was too busy living, chum. Only one-legged men or

fellows with no arms should marry. No sensible man with guts should ever marry. I've had a life of freedom. You can't have that with a woman around your neck trying to get you to wear a collar and tie. Women are for those who need them, chum, for the weaklings who want their three meals on time and to be canceled out from the real living. This is the real living, out here like this, with no one trying to make you a nicer person than you want to be. Why? Are you married?"

"I was, but it didn't work. I pulled out, but she still writes to me. She was O.K. but I was no good at being her wife."

"There you are, you see," said Gilligan. "You're not an ant-man, that's what it means. You were all wrong to marry, that's what it means. You're a man of action. The only action you can get in marriage is about who said what last Tuesday and why you shouldn't have said it. I've watched married people. They give you a pain in the neck. There's not one married couple who aren't fighting about something. Is that why you're out here, getting over a woman?"

"I don't need to get over a woman. They have to get over me," Muller replied. 'I wonder why we don't get on better, Gilligan and me? I mean we're quite like each other in a lot of ways, only I've got real guts and he hasn't. I know this guy has a crack in him. I'm certain of it. He's a softy inside. You can feel it. All that crap about liking elephants. Not shooting them because he actually likes them. Am I supposed to swallow that stuff? How old am I supposed to be? Liking elephants! Yeah? Huh!'

"You never shot an elephant, Gill? I mean you've never gone after one and shot it, because you always liked

them? But you don't feel like that about other animals,
you mean? You just like elephants and won't shoot them.
Is that it?"

"That's it, more or less," Gilligan said, looking at him
hard for a moment. Gilligan's pace had never changed,
whether on sand or over rocks, and he looked as fresh as
when they had started.

"With me it'd be all or nothing," said Muller. "I mean
I'd shoot everything or let everything live. I don't get
that one about elephants and shoot the rest."

"There are plenty of things you wouldn't understand,
I expect," said Gilligan. "Why? Have you another theory?
Surely you must have another theory. You're fond of
theories, like all Yanks, I suppose. What's your theory this
time, about me and elephants?"

"You've never shot one yet?"

"Never."

"And you don't want to shoot this one, that one that
killed your buddy?"

"Ah! I'd shoot this one, but you're going to shoot it
instead. That's why you're here, isn't it? Why, do you feel
you mightn't be up to it? I'll shoot it if you like."

"Now you're trying to ride me again, you see? Always
trying to ride somebody. *I* have no worry about taking on
an elephant, or anything else either, don't you worry
yourself. *I* don't have any *thing* about anything like that.
It all comes in one package, to me. *I* don't have to worry
about elephants. You send me the elephant and I'll knock
it down. *I* don't have any reason to *like* elephants."

"What do you mean by that, *you* don't have any reason
to *like* elephants? What am I supposed to make out of
that?"

"You can make anything you like, pal. Anything. It's for free." 'That jolted him all right, that one. He looks like somebody gave him a kick in the ass. Yeah, he took that one down where it hurts.' "And as far as I'm concerned anything you say is O.K. with me, because I don't feel like fighting about nothing right now. O.K.?"

"I'm not trying to fight, Muller. It's you who like to fight. Feeling all right? Do you find it hotter than you expected?"

"*I'm* all right, pal, thank you. Don't you worry about me. I'm O.K. Anything you can do I can do better. Anything. Don't you start worrying about how I'm feeling."

"Touchy chap, my God. Let's drop the subject."

"Fine."

The country here became harder, low but steep ridges covered with white rocks. Muller felt as if someone had stuffed a hot coal into his head and he had a pain behind his eyes, like a bar of hot metal just behind the eyeballs. Was he soft? Was he really as tough as Gilligan and the Africans walking behind them? It was much harder going than he had imagined and he was having to remind himself that the elephant was going to be worth it.

II. The Wilderness

16

ONLY THE SMALL HUNTING TRIBES came up here into this isolated country. They came to make their arrow poison and to hunt. It was one of the last free territories left to the indigenous hunters and had only remained so because to get to it was too difficult, and it was still out of reach of the white man. Only the odd Gilligan had come up here, the kind of white man who liked hard country and preferred to go as far as he could away from his fellows.

A small aging hunter called Gavai was squatting over a bird trap he was making when he heard a sound some distance off. He moved behind a bush and looked through it and saw Chongu trotting down the side of a ridge. Gavai sat down behind the bush and studied Chongu, remembering him by his movements and by the *feel* of what he looked like, recalling him from years ago when they had gone after elephant with a white man, and how

they had buried another white man. Then Chongu and
the white man had vanished out of his life, and now here
was Chongu coming back as if everything had been
yesterday. He hoped Chongu would have tobacco on
him.

'If he has no tobacco then I will not speak a single word
to him,' Gavai vowed, fearful that there would be no tobacco. 'I will give no assistance, reply to no questions. I
will run away.' He craved for some tobacco, and he had
a small metal pipe hanging on a cord round his neck, a
pipe that had not issued smoke for more than he could
bear to remember.

There would be a white man with Chongu, but he
could see nobody but Chongu, and Chongu had now
disappeared and would be climbing the opposite ridge.
It would not be long before he appeared on the top.
Chongu came onto the top of the ridge, still trotting, and
then started down the side. There were three more ridges
to cover. 'If he has no tobacco I will just turn my back
on him and leave him,' Gavai vowed. 'Only one unde-
serving of help would come up here without tobacco. He
must have tobacco. If he has a white man with him then
there should be tobacco, so I will not turn away from
him if he has no tobacco. I will wait for his white man.
But if he too is without tobacco then I shall give no help,
no word, nothing. Why should I? Here I am, poor, and
getting old too, wifeless, without tobacco. I would like a
hut full of tobacco, full to the top, and I would smoke it
all for myself. I wouldn't give any away to anybody.
Not a speck of it. Why didn't I when I sold those tusks,
why didn't I buy a lot of tobacco and store it up, instead
of wasting the money drinking and buying presents for

people I didn't know in that town by the river? What fools we are, we people who live in the forest. No cunning, no thought. Here he is, on the ridge. I'm in such a state that I might kill him if he has no tobacco.'

Gavai was trembling as Chongu drew nearer, terrified of finding that Chongu had no tobacco with him. He wanted to run and meet Chongu, to find out, but he sat out of habit and watched from cover, studying Chongu carefully. He had not seen a stranger up here for many years and had it not been for the aching longing for tobacco he would have slipped away into the bush, but he was tied to the outside world by strings of tobacco, just as others of his group were tied to it by desire for coffee and matches and medicine; so Chongu was carrying a thread to him, Gavai, who was craving for a smoke at his cold pipe.

He was small and black, and beginning to wrinkle as fast as his short crimped hair was grizzling with time. He watched Chongu fixedly, almost fanatically, as if willing him to have tobacco. Unable to control himself any longer, Gavai rushed out from the bush and began to shout, "Tobacco. Tobacco. Have you brought tobacco with you? Here, it is Gavai, who knew you once. But have you tobacco?" He stood to listen.

"I have tobacco," Chongu shouted. Gavai gave a short screech of joy and began to hop from one foot to the other all along the top of the ridge, punching the air to the rhythm of his dance, singing, "My pipe shall burn again and I am ready to die after it. Quite ready. Give me the tobacco, stranger, and let me smoke it for you." Chongu stood and watched until the old man had finished his ceremony of joy.

Gavai, with uncertain nervous fingers, undid his pipe from the cord around his neck and then held it out to Chongu. "Fill it," he said. "To the top. Then talk to me. I will tell you anything you want to know that I may know. But fill it first. To the top." He sat down and folded his arms and watched Chongu squat and take his leather bag from his shoulder strap. There was so much tobacco in the bag that Gavai came on his hands and knees to look at it. Chongu let him feel it, let him hold a handful and fondle it and smell it.

"How did you know I was here dying for want of tobacco?" Gavai asked him.

"We have to know these things, old fellow," Chongu said gravely. "If we did not know these things we would be running around starving like yourself. To the brainy and the knowing go the jobs with the white men. That is the way it is, old fellow. Here is your pipe. And *kibrit* to light it." He tossed a box of matches to Gavai. Then he sat and enjoyed watching the enjoyment of the old withered man as the first clouds of rank smoke came out of the burning tobacco. The sigh of the old man made him laugh.

"Now you are happier, old fellow," he said.

"Now I am happier," said Gavai. "Speak. I'm listening to you. Speak. How far have you traveled to here, and why? What have you come for this time?"

"For the elephant that killed the white man that time when everyone then living was younger than he is now. You are getting old."

"Time has passed, that's why. That elephant is a long way from here, and I will not go near it for you, unless

you give me a great deal of tobacco. But I know where
it is. It is a far way from where we are sitting now."

"How far?"

"As far as it would take twenty of those sticks to dry
in your hand, one after the other." Gavai pointed to some
green bushes nearby. "Three nights sleeping out it would
take you before you came to where it lives now. And
there is a young elephant with it, a friend. And beyond
that again is a herd of them. It is a long way."

"When did you last see it?"

"When I was staying with the group of Gandu, teaching his young men to make arrow poison." He turned
and pointed with his chin to the far hills behind him.
"Gandu has soil with maize in it, near a spring, and I ate
there for ten nights running. I was sick after it, I ate too
much. And the elephant came when I was there and tore
up Gandu's *shamba*, and we all laughed, for you know
it is not right for us in our group to grow things. This
elephant is mad. We all ran. Gandu offered me much to
go after it with the young men and kill it, but I would
sooner live on until it is the right time for me to go. I
could not kill that elephant. It would kill me. It listens
and it sees and it thinks. Didn't it kill that white man
that time? I left it. It is best to let a white man kill it
from afar with a gun. Where is your white man? Tell me
everything. Everything." He puffed smoke into the hot,
still air of the late afternoon. The sun was falling over the
far mountain and the sky was filling with a reddish-
bronze haze, and although it had been quiet before it was
now utterly silent, that silence which seems to be commanded by the dying sun over wilderness.

"How much do you remember of that last time when we passed through here, and I stayed at the camp and you were there with me, and the white men went ahead, and one came back, and then you went forward with me and helped to bury the one who was killed by the elephant? How much of that do you remember?" Chongu watched the old man steadily with his long, black sharp eyes.

"Everything," said Gavai.

"Then forget everything," said Chongu. "It is the same white man with me, and he will not remember you, and it would be best if you did not remember anything. He was not himself after that white man was killed."

"He ran away. My son watched him from the trees. He saw everything. That shows you what kind of an elephant it is. And now he is back to kill it. It is unlucky. He was right to run away. No one will kill that elephant. He should be left alone. He has a brain like I have, that elephant. I too would run away."

"So would I, if nobody was watching," said Chongu. This convulsed the old man, who took his pipe out of his mouth to laugh properly, bending forward and squealing exaggeratedly in the way of his people. Chongu, a half smile on his thick, finely shaped mouth, watched him until the convulsion was over. Then he continued, "But white men are not like that, and mine is worse than most of them. Do you understand? You must forget everything. Mine ran away. I heard all about it before we left here. Mine does not know that I know. Good. That is the way it should be. So forget everything. Appear as a stranger. And take us to the elephant. There are two white men this time again. They have words all day. They compete. They quarrel. It is terrible for all of us.

And we have a Somali with us. He has caused trouble, but without meaning to, which is not usual for a Somali, is it, to cause trouble without planning it?" This again convulsed Gavai who, caught with smoke in his lungs, choked, sprang up, and ran about coughing with laughter while tears came into his eyes. When it was over he came back and sat down, wiping his eyes with his black, wrinkled, hard hand.

"You are very sharp with that tongue of yours," he said, cackling again. "Now, this Somali. Is he of the noble tribes or one of the small, blackish ones, like me? A noble, of course?"

"A noble."

"Well, first the elephant. I don't want to go near it. I have told you that. And now this Somali. That is as bad as the elephant. He will kick me and I will be able to do nothing in return to him. It is better that I vanish. I want nothing to do with this business. And the white men quarrel. Why do they quarrel? What is it about?"

"They are both proud men. Aganaza, the headman, says that they are similar men, men of ability and neither likes the other. All I know is that I keep as far away as possible. How much tobacco would you want to put up with the Somali, and to take us to the elephant?"

"More than you have with you."

"A man's eyes cannot see everything another man has," Chongu said reprovingly. "There is more in the world than your two eyes take in, old fellow."

"Very well, then where is it, the rest of the tobacco?"

"In the box with the white men. Plenty of it. As much as you can smoke in your time left to you. Now what are you waiting for? Are you agreed?"

"I will trust you because I remember you," Gavai said, puffing at the pipe. "It is done. I'll take you to the elephant."

"You have done well for yourself, old fellow. You have done a right thing there. Here." He tossed the bag of tobacco to the old man, who caught it with one swift movement of his hand. "You can keep the bag as well. Show me a good place near water for a camp, before night."

"I will take you there," Gavai said, rising and slinging the bag on his shoulder, a contented man now. "Over there on that ridge is a spring of fresh, clear water, good for a white man's soft belly. There is other water here on this ridge, but the white man would be squatting all day if he drank that. Come, I will take you to the spring. There are trees as well." He looked at Chongu. "Have these white men got bottles of drink with them?"

"They have."

"Will you steal one for me? Just one?"

"If everything goes well and you are as useful as you were once, I'll steal one for you at the end of everything. That is a promise."

"You will not regret that promise. I'm your man, young one. None better."

17

ONLY JAMA WAS UNAFFECTED by that terrific march on the first day, for he was born to this, this saunter in the fierce sun, and he was as fresh when he ended the day as when he began it. Gilligan had nearly killed himself by all appearances, by the way he was lying on his back on his camp bed, pale and exhausted looking, though he had not been the first to stop for a rest. The other Bwana had had to give in first and suggest a rest. Jama had grinned behind his hand while he watched this.

Muller had gone mentally through a long and complicated series of rehearsed scenes, all of them to do with suggesting a rest, until he found one which satisfied him, and it was so simple he could not think why he had not thought of it long ago during the early hours of this day's torment. He had stumbled on a small rock, most realistically, and had grasped his ankle, swearing, and had sat down to nurse it, in obvious pain. But Gilligan was not fooled.

"Your ankle's all right. Come on. We've got bloody miles to go yet, chum. You can get all the rest you want tonight in camp. Once you sit down on a long march you stiffen up. Come on. You haven't hurt yourself." Seething, but saying nothing about it, Muller would not get up. He was too happy. His body was so grateful for this sit down that he felt it was going to break into delirious song. He had never been so exhausted in his life before, and he knew Gilligan had driven himself too far as well. Gilligan looked drawn and ill, so far gone in fact that Muller, after studying him, burst out into hysterical laughter. Gilligan sat down then and looked at him. The Africans sank down into the grass too, all except Jama, who stayed on his feet and went on studying the two white men, whose feud was fascinating him.

"By God, you're glad I stumbled that time, aren't you," Muller said, showing his temper in the glinting of his hot gray eyes. "You're all in. Don't kid me. You look like something before the mortician gets through with the paint. So you're O.K. now. You can have a rest, and it's on me." He thought he had made it sound good, convincing.

"I don't know what you're talking about, Muller," Gilligan said, rising to his feet, his body screaming for just a little more rest, just a few more minutes, but he could not afford to give in to it. On. On. "Come on, Muller. We've got miles to go. You'll have to harden up. This is nothing to the country we've got to go through further on." Never before on a march had he driven himself like this, and he was feeling worried by the way his body was responding. It was tiring, and it was begging for respite. He would give it none. On. "Come on, Muller," he pleaded insultingly, "Get up. The blacks are watching you."

"—— the blacks," Muller yelled at him. "What about my ankle?" It was no good. He had not fooled Gilligan, who was looking at him with cold, cynical eyes while Muller, in despair, pulled himself to his feet. His legs felt as if they were going to collapse. He pushed one leg forward and then dragged the other after it, walking.

"That's it," Gilligan said. "Don't give in. Remember the blacks are watching you all the time. I never let a black see me beat. Never. They respect you for it too, chum. That's right. Step it out. You're soft, that's all it is. Before this safari's over you'll be as fit as I am, and that's fit, chum. But I got that way through driving myself. O.K. now? Feeling all right?"

"Shut your goddam yap," Muller snapped at him. He was walking well again now, but his mind was not willing and he was having to screw up his will, and was managing it. "You mean to tell me that you spend your life trying to outwalk your Africans? That it's not just a white war with you, it includes the Africans as well? You mean you think *they're* watching you too?"

"I've walked Africans off their feet," said Gilligan, "and they don't forget it. You can laugh. But it's paid me. What I'm waiting for is to see that Somali, Jama, beg for mercy, and he's going to, chum. He's going to. He's too bloody proud. These Somalis think they're tougher and braver than everyone in the world, but by the time I've finished with this one he'll never want to see or hear of me again. He's looking all right now, but I'll finish him, by Christ, as sure as my name's Gilligan. He'll wish he was back there where I threw him into the bush."

"Listen, you're crazy. Do you know that? I mean really crazy, mad, pal. Did anyone ever tell you that, that you're mad?" They looked into each other's eyes and Gilligan was laughing.

"You don't understand people like me, Muller," he said. "That's all it is. Some men pile up money in offices. I don't. I go after other things. My name's known from Addis Ababa to Lourenco Marques. I'm not fooling, you know. I'm known, boy, as the tough one, and one who's not afraid of anything, and I'm proud of that. Why shouldn't I be? Show me *one* man, I mean Man, not one of these bloody ant-men, but show me one Man who wouldn't like to change places with me. I know, chum, that you came into this safari determined to get me down. Why? I don't know. But you're wasting your time. You'll never do it, and you've seen today that you can't. Give it up. Be yourself."

"I'm telling you that you're crazy, mad," Muller said, "and I'm telling you something else. You've tried to walk me onto my face today. But you won't do it, pal. I can do anything you can do, and better. You want it this way, right, we're having it this way."

"That shows spirit anyway," Gilligan said. "I like that. You're glad now, aren't you, that I made you get up back there? You were giving in, weren't you? Don't do it. And remember the blacks are watching all the time." They were gripped in the same mania together now, full of sun.

Was he mad after all? Gilligan wondered. It was only with other white men that this thought came up. When he was in the bush with Africans he never felt this doubt, never wondered if he was anything but normal. Yet sometimes, like today, he found himself doubting, wondering if he was quite sane after all.

When Gilligan and Muller were lying on their camp beds, whiskies close to hand, and the big fire in the center of the camp was showering red sparks from its flames, Jama, Aganaza, and the two skinners stood around the fire and drank tea. Jama was having another argument with Aganaza, about white men.

"You are an ignorant man, Aganaza," Jama said. "You have these stupid, womanish, ideas in your head, but you know nothing really. Listen to me for a while and learn something. I was a soldier for years and I know something about fear and courage. These two white men now, they are only out to see what they can do. I've been watching them. Your own white man, Gilligan, is too hot, too proud. He was going to strike me. No one has ever been allowed to hit me. I would not let him do it. So he sacked me. He hates this other white man because he gave me work again. His pride is hurt. And here's another thing. One of them is an American, and they're very rich indeed. Your fellow has no money. Even I have more money in Mogadishu than he has in his home. His home is the home of a poor man. I had a look at it. But money isn't everything. Gilligan is proud of being strong. The question now is, Which of the two of them is the strongest?" He looked at Aganaza who was listening to every word and weighing what he was hearing.

"It is well known, Jama, that all Somalis have brains like you, full of *fitina* and trouble. I am telling you that my Bwana will not stand for it from you. Look out for yourself. He does not like Somalis. He had trouble with them before. He shot some of them, people like you who think they are like white men and come shouting and threatening into the camp. The Bwana will not listen to it. If you go about the way you do much longer he will shoot you. Each man has his place. Why I, who have worked for him for many years, would not dare behave as you do with your big mouth. And remember this, I am the senior man in this camp under the white man. Do not upset me with your mouth and your ways, Jama. I am sick of your ways."

"You say your Bwana shot some Somalis. When was this?"

"*My* Bwana? Isn't he yours too? Don't you take pay from him again since he told the other white man what was what?"

"All right, he is my Bwana for now too. But these Somalis he shot. Are you lying to me?"

"I would not waste my time lying to somebody like you. He shot impudent Somalis like you, who came shouting into the camp. You are bad people. You think you are better than everyone else."

"We *are* better than everyone else. Better than white men and all the black men, and everybody knows it. No white man likes to believe it, so they sack us and throw us off the truck in the middle of the bush. The other white man isn't like that. He rescued me. He valued me. He knows I am intelligent and reliable man, not one of these brainless slaves like yourselves, here, all of you are slaves. That is the way you are made. If it had not been for the white men coming to this land, we Somalis would have come down here and those we did not kill we would have chained up for work." Jama was exalting himself, quivering with it.

"How is it that you never say these things to the white men?" Aganaza asked insinuatingly. "How is it you have all this big talk here by the fire, and when the white man is close by you are like us, respectful and obedient? How is this, big mouth?"

"Be careful. I will stand for so much from a slave, Aganaza. You saw me draw my knife and you saw your Bwana draw back. He changed his mind. He did not strike me after all. He respects me for that. When this safari is finished I leave. I will not work for your Bwana even if I was dying of hunger. This is an unhappy camp. Everyone is unhappy, because of your Bwana. And he is only a poor man, your Bwana. Why should he be proud? Why should he behave like a king? He has nothing. It is the American who has the money, and he does not shout as loud as Gilligan. I have never seen a camp as unhappy as this one. Never. I have come low in the world, working for Gilligan. Before this I worked for rich men, men who would throw money away and think nothing of it. Your Bwana respects me now. I taught him that. Work and pay. That is the arrangement, and no using the fist." He raved on for a while, all listening to him in wonder, for they never expressed themselves in this way. There was always something astonishing in the massive vanity and speechmaking of the Somalis, and in their vindictiveness and their readiness to show spirit. They were ungovernable, and resented because of it. They thought nothing good could come of anybody who was not a Somali. Jama said that should Gilligan ever threaten him again he would know what to do.

"And what would that be, that thing you would know what to do?" Aganaza asked, fearfully, and smiling with it.

"Your Bwana will never shoot me, as you say he shot other Somalis," Jama said, intoxicated with himself now. "Never. But these two white men are lying on their beds, worn out by their trying to down each other, and now you are trying to down me, Aganaza, which is impossible for a slave man to do to a Somali. More tea."

"Get it yourself."

"Then I will do without it, but I will remember you."

"And I will remember you."

"Enough."

"Enough it is. Let us say no more. There is enough trouble in this camp without a Somali making more."

"There is a curse on this camp," Jama declaimed. "But it is not on me. I am free. I have no curse on me. And here is another thing. I am not tired after today and the rest of you are. I am a Somali. We never get tired."

"Tell us no more. Enough."

"Enough, then."

18

HE HAD OVERDONE IT, and he knew it as he lay in the red flickering darkness and watched the sparks bursting from the crackling logs on the fire. He could see Muller moving about, smoking, talking to Jama. Yes, he had done himself up with today's effort, and like all very healthy people when faced with pain or illness, or the sign of age, he was fretting about it. He had never felt so done up as he felt just now. Thank God for whisky. He drank the one off he had and wanted another. He did not want to move, but he had been lying down here for nearly an hour since they had got into camp, and there was Muller, up and about, and he knew he could not afford to lie down much longer. Muller would notice it at once and be one up on him again. Why couldn't the bastard lie still for just another half-hour? It was all deliberate, of course, just one more effort to show who was who. Right. Very well, chum. If that was the way he wanted it, very well.

Suppressing a groan, he got up from the bed, racked with pains in his joints and muscles. There was no doubt about it but it had been a big day all right, the biggest he had ever done, come to think it over. He was proud of himself, and he was paying. He knew he had really shaken Muller with today's effort. He, Gilligan, had shown no signs of weakening, and he must not show any now. Up. Get up. He was up, walking across to the fire, strolling, glass in hand.

"Aganaza. *Leta* whisky *na maji.*" Aganaza filled the glass for him. "Everything all right, Aganaza?"

"All going well, Bwana." Aganaza smiled.

"And that Somali? No *fitina*? Not making any trouble?"

"Plenty of talk, Bwana, the usual Somali talk."

"Yes. Talk. I know it. Keep your eye on him. Don't let him boss you about. You're headman in this camp, and don't let him forget it. Bwana Muller tired, do you think?"

"Very tired, Bwana. He can hardly walk."

"He's soft, that's all. He'll soon be hard. None of them are as tough as your Bwana. None of them."

"*Wewe Bwana Mkubwa sana, Bwana,*" Aganaza said, meaning most of it.

"Too bloody true I'm the big Bwana," Gilligan said, thoughtful.

"*Mkubwa sana sana,*" Aganaza said, overdoing it, yet meaning most of it, but even Gilligan knew when enough praise was enough.

"That'll do," he said. "*Natosha.* Get on with the dinner."

"*Ndio, Bwana.*" Aganaza went back to his kitchen fire.

"Trying to grease me up, you bastard," Gilligan said,

smiling fondly after Aganaza. "I know I'm good but I can praise myself as well. Funny about the blacks, simple people, saying what they feel all the time." It could be embarrassing at times.

Muller approached him. "Feel better now?" he asked Gilligan.

"I never felt anything else. Why? You look pretty played out. Like to take it easier tomorrow? We can, you know, if you like. A few rests. Like that?"

Muller was feeling ill. He thought he was running a slight temperature. He drank down his whisky and called for another. Aganaza came swiftly out of the shadows, bottle and jug in hand. "You know, Gilligan," Muller was saying, "you could be a great guy. You could be liked. You've got what it takes, but you're not sure of it." Muller was swaying about. His face shone with sweat.

"You look rather ill to me, Muller," Gilligan said with real concern.

"Let me speak, will you, pal? I want to tell you something. I want to get something straight. It's this. Make it tough. As tough as you like. And quit hoping. You'll never see me down. Never. Make it real tough and watch me. Watch *me*. And watch yourself too. Think it over. You think you can kid me you strolled in here tonight feeling great? You were almost on your knees, pal. Admit it. On your knees. You *fell* down onto your goddam bed. And you looked like you hadn't slept for a whole. year. Is it worth it? Is it worth it at your age? You're pushing me, but you're killing yourself. You met Mr. Right this time. I'll see you out if you want to. Make it tough. Make it tough." He looked like a man with heat-stroke.

"Are you hungry?" Gilligan was patient now, and grim.

"Don't dodge the point. Don't start anything new. Stick to the subject. I want to try and like you, do you know that? But you really get a guy down, Gilligan. I'll never forget you. This is childish, all this muscle stuff, but I'm with you now, right down the line. I'm with you."

Sweated out as he was after the killing day he had had, exhaustion had made Muller feel lightheaded, and as always after a day of tremendous exertion in the tropics, the whisky hit him harder than it normally would. He was half drunk, and emotionally on edge after the day of grim and wearing endurance which he had let Gilligan force upon him. Gilligan himself could hardly stand, but he played the patient and amused listener to Muller's almost ridiculous ravings.

"Africa's a curious place, Muller. It makes everything behave strangely, especially white people." Gilligan lit a cigarette with a shaking hand. God, but he felt old right now. "You're behaving strangely yourself. You'll get used to it. Like me. Have another big whisky and stop trying to quarrel with me."

Muller watched Gilligan's eyes, trying to trust him, to believe in this innocent concern for their relationship after the long day of combat they had spent together, after the way they had driven each other under the sun.

He smiled tiredly. "O.K. Let's have another snort."

"That's better," said Gilligan. He was feeling the whisky, in his head, in his shaky hands. But he knew his age had been made frightened and angry by today's punishment. He wanted to be friendly but he could not afford it. Yet he would try.

They drank several whiskies and fell into the curious friendly enmity, all touchy and prickly, which they were now becoming used to. They got rather drunk and began an argument about tactics in battle, about how a company should attack a ridge with bunkers in it, and whether bombing and shell fire was really a help in jungle country, tearing down the cover as it did. Muller insisted on treating Gilligan as old-fashioned, out of date, from the First World War, and Gilligan kept on, indignantly, reminding Muller that, as well as the First World War, he had served three years in the jungle war of Burma. Muller only paused to listen, suspiciously, when Gilligan claimed he had killed a bloody sight more Japanese than Muller. Things had been going almost pleasantly, and now Gilligan was being Gilligan again.

"Now we know," Muller said. "Now you've said it. Now we know what I suspected. I *knew* you must have killed more Japs than I had. I knew it. You're lying to me, pal. But it's O.K. Just admit you've been lying to me and we'll pass on. Next question, please."

"Don't you say that to me." Gilligan clenched his fists.

"You didn't believe *me*, did you, when I told you I had killed forty-six Japs? Why should I believe you?"

"Let's drop the subject, please," Gilligan was icy and dignified.

"Sure, let's drop it. I'm for that. Drop it. Give me your hand." Muller held out his hand for Indian wrestling, something he had never done before, and, furious, Gilligan seized his hand. They were too drunk to perform properly, both of them pushing and pulling, accusing each other of cheating and pushing and taking mean advantage. Aganaza came up to say that dinner was ready and was told to go to hell, and then to bring some more whisky. When Aganaza came with a new bottle of whisky Gilligan pulled the cork out and threw it away, saying, "Down the bloody hatch. To the bottom," and filled their glasses. They gripped each other's hands again, laughing, and started to strain. They finished the bottle of whisky, quite drunk. The camp was silent and the enormous silver moon was high in a cloudless purple sky. Some hyenas were gulping and howling not far away.

"All day tomorrow without any rest at all, that's what I want," Muller said belligerently when they gave up the useless effort to best each other at Indian wrestling. "All day, dawn to dusk, and no rest. I want to show you, pal, that you took on the very best when you started on me. Dawn to dusk. Right?"

"Dawn to dusk it'll be," Gilligan shouted, banging the table with his fist. His back was hurting and he had been worrying about it and he was all on edge. "If that's what you want that's what we'll have. I'm game, chum. You've upset me, and we'll have it your way. Dawn to dusk."

They fought to help each other to their beds. Gilligan could hardly move his legs. He was trying to push Muller to his bed and Muller was pushing him. Aganaza came and separated them, taking Gilligan to his bed, and then went after the reeling Muller and guided him to his. Muller fell face down, asleep before he hit the sheet.

Aganaza hummed to himself, as usual when he was worried. Tomorrow, as always after a drunken night, Bwana Gilligan would be at his worst. Nothing would please him. He was so much better when he was alone, Bwana Gilligan, but every time he had another *Mzungu* with him on safari there was always trouble. The American *Mzungu* was snoring loudly.

Aganaza went to the table and picked up the whisky bottle. There was a glassful in the bottom of it. He took it with him to his bedroll and sat down to drink it. He felt sorry for Bwana Gilligan, and he could not think why he should feel this. At times like this Bwana Gilligan made him sad. And Bwana Gilligan was getting old. He had watched him tonight and had seen how stiff he was. Time ate men up, and there was a village to go to and become old in, but Bwana Gilligan could not do that. What would happen, then, to Bwana Gilligan? He had no money. He was as poor as one of those old Dutchmen. There would always be a place in Aganaza's village for Bwana Gilligan when he got too old to walk in the bush, but Bwana Gilligan would not accept such hospitality. But Aganaza knew he would be happy there, far from the city, old and decaying into death. He had spent so long with Bwana Gilligan that he knew him like a brother. And tonight he felt afraid for him. He sat in the moonlight, the bottle in his hand, wondering why he felt afraid for Bwana Gilligan.

19

"You NEVER KNOW what you can do until you have to do it. You make that effort and you win, and it had to be made."

It was pitch dark, warm and still, and Gilligan could hear Muller moving about the camp. He had awakened out of one of his strange, terrifying dreams in which he was running away on silent feet, through darkness, and a voice was chanting, "That's it. Faster. Nobody's seen you. Faster. You'll make it and nobody'll see. Everything's going fine. Just keep at it. Faster. Faster." It was Muller's voice which had awakened him, Muller calling softly to Jama. Immediately he knew what was afoot. Muller was getting everything ready to do one of his surprise readinesses on him again.

Gilligan could hardly move. His body felt as if it had been on a rack. A panic and a fear fell upon him and he gripped the side of the camp bed and started to get up.

136

Aganaza must have heard him, Aganaza who knew what was going on, knew that Muller was going to do his Bwana one in the eye again. He had been standing nearby, wondering if his Bwana was going to wake up in time.

"That you, Aganaza?"

"*Ndio, Bwana.*"

"Help me up. I'm a bit stiff. Get hold of my hand and pull." All this in a whisper.

"Are you ill, Bwana?"

"No. Just stiff, that's all. Don't chatter. Get hold of my hand and help me up."

He almost cried aloud as Aganaza pulled him off the bed; every muscle and tendon felt like pieces of hot metal bending unwillingly in his flesh. But once he was on his feet the pain went down. He swayed slightly, summoned up the will into the citadel, and walked. Agony. Wear it off. Punish the body. Drive the whimpering flesh.

Once, half mad with malaria, he had walked through a wilderness in which he had been followed by tribesmen who were waiting to see him drop so they could glide in for the pickings, his watch, his rifle, his this and his that. But he had gone through, won. Another time he had gone far from his truck after meat, got caught in darkness, and got lost. Two days of wandering terror trying to pull him down in a loss of courage, into giving up, and finally he had found water and had lived, and had got himself together and had started all over again, and had found his truck. Again, in the Kedong in the old days, he had fallen down a hill and had broken his two right lower ribs. He never forgot the agony, the delirium of that walk back, and he had won. What about Burma? What about that time he had been cut off by Japs and had walked his way out, right through them, sucked to weakness by leeches?

He walked up and down in the darkness while Aganaza watched him. Then the hangover which had lain behind the panic of this stiffness came up and hit him in the skull. Nausea overtook him. He reeled. Aganaza stepped forward and caught him, steadied him, and knowingly, let him go again just in time, just before the Bwana snapped at him.

"*Funga vitu yote,*" Gilligan said to Aganaza. "*Funga safari.* We're moving." He could hardly dress himself. He tottered about until he was dressed. Then he felt a little better and sat down.

"By God, I'm in a bad way," he said in a whisper to himself. "I feel done. That's that whisky. I hit it last night too hard. I'm not old, though, don't start that one. That is just not true, chum. What about old Ridley, at eighty he was on his last safari? What about old Two Bottle Jackson, who drove a trade truck until he was seventy-five, and could walk younger men off their feet?" No. It was not age. God blast it, he was only fifty-seven. Fifty-seven. But he had overdone it yesterday, there was no getting away from that. It was a long time since he had done a walk like yesterday's effort. But today was going to be all out, "And you'll see, after two miles every ache will be gone and I'll be in there showing that bastard what's what!" But he had never felt like this before after a day's walk. No, it was all that whisky on top.

"What the hell are you doing, Muller? Are you ready or are you going to start that breakfast lark of yours?" He roared the words cheerfully and defiantly into the darkness. "Hurry up with that tea, Aganaza," he said in a low

voice. "And give me two aspirins. No, make it four."
Aganaza came rushing with a cup of tea and a bottle of
aspirins. Muller appeared out of the darkness.

"Drinking tea, eh?" he said. "How are you feeling,
old-timer?"

"Cut out the old-timer. I'm all right, thank you. In
fact I never felt better. And you?"

"I could lift a horse, one in each hand. Now, listen,
how far is this camp you sent Chongu to? How many
hours march is it?"

"We can make it by midday tomorrow. Why?"

"I want to make it in one go, tonight."

"You don't know what you're talking about, Muller.
We're doing fine as it is. We've got plenty of time. What
do you want to make the camp tonight for?"

"I just want to do it, that's why. Too much for you,
is that it? Just say the word. I'm O.K. Are you up to it
or not?"

"There's no question of my being up to it or not."
Gilligan was snarling now. "It's a tough march. And I
don't see the sense of it. Dawn to dusk you wanted, didn't
you? You can write home about that, can't you? Why this
sudden urge to do one and a half day's march in one go?
As things are if we walk from dawn to dusk as you've
pestered me into doing already, you'll be done at the end
of it, I can tell you. You know how you felt yesterday
after only a few hours. What's this new idea all about?"

"Just say if you're not up to it, pal. I want to really
try myself all out. And don't get mad at me. If you feel
like doing it, then I'm all for it. If you want to back
down, just say. It's O.K. with me."

"There's no bloody question of *backing down*." Gilligan was in a passion, on his feet, his cup of tea slopping over. You're out of your mind, Muller." He felt afraid, as if some kind of devil was grinning between them both.

"All right. So you don't want to do it? Is that right?"

"Who said I don't want to do it? I'm just saying it's not necessary, that's all I'm saying. Look, I know you're tough. I know you're all man. Fine. But you don't have to kill yourself, do you?" 'This fellow wants to kill me,' Gilligan thought.

"I told you to quit worrying about my health, pal. I want to know if you're able to do this all-out march or not. If you're not able to do it, then say so. But quit the stalling, will you? Will you or won't you make the camp with me tonight?"

Gilligan made his mind up. Have it out, to the very end. There was no use dodging this one. He was with a madman, a fellow who drove himself and then jeered if everyone else could not keep up, a head case in fact. He felt his will and his temper clench in him like a fist.

"Right," he said, rubbing his hands, rejuvenated with the rage he felt. "Right, Muller. We'll do it. Packed?"

"Packed? I've been waiting, pal. I've been ready for an hour or more while you're drinking your tea. Let's go."

Jama, cursing in Arabic and Somali, had dragged himself out of his warm blanket in a daze after much shaking by Aganaza.

"What is the matter with these Europeans?" he snarled. "It is night. Night. Are we to march now, in this night-time?"

"Dress quickly," Aganaza said. "They're ready to move off."

"But where is my tea?"

"Remember, you are a Somali, a warrior," Aganaza hissed at him. "Why should you complain when even we slaves are ready to march?" He left Jama and went to rouse the others. With their rifles on their shoulders Muller and Gilligan had already started off, stumbling about on the rocks in the darkness.

Muller, who always looked on sleep as a thief who tried to steal a third of every day from a man's short life, could do with little of it. As soon as he had opened his eyes in the darkness he had thought, 'Yesterday has to be wiped out. Yesterday I was chicken.' He had suffered much in remembering the mean little way he had pretended to have hurt his foot so that he could have a rest. That was weakness, humiliating the way he had lied to get a rest. Gilligan was dominating him all the way, making him conform to unspoken standards, causing him to lie so as to get a rest, and yet he knew that Gilligan's standards were his own as well. Trying to understand it brought on doubts and these were always swept away by anger. 'It's got to be wiped out. And today I'll do it. Today I'll walk until he drops. It's the only way to finish this thing once and for all.'

It was no use trying to pretend that he was not enjoying it. He was. But this kind of thing should be done before judges, with referees and rules. As it was now, there was only a feeling between them that each was the better man, and there was only one way of getting around that. That was for one of them to fall down, beaten, and then the other could forgive, could help him to his feet, and then, well, shake hands and call it a day.

'It's crazy, but he makes it seem normal. Today I'm going all out, right down the line, to the finish. And I've got what it takes. This guy has to meet someone who is really tops, someone he will never forget. He's had everything all his own way for years and you can see it in everything he does and says. I never met anyone who brings the worst out in me the way he does.' And he knew he did the same thing to Gilligan. 'How far's this camp of his? Walk to it without a break, that's the thing to do. One epic march, all out.' He had jumped out of his bed, groaning with the unexpected onset of pains in his muscles. Ten minutes walking would clear that. The thing now was this—was he ready and set for one all-out killing march, one that would finish Gilligan's smug watchfulness? Yes. And raring to go.

As they made their way over the rocks in the darkness, the heat becoming thicker and closer to the skin, Gilligan made several grumbling remarks.

"It's your choice, this, don't forget that. God knows what goes on in that mind of yours, Muller. I don't. But you've asked for it. You've forced this on us. And we'll do it. I'm not going to have you gassing your head off in Nairobi about what you did to me and so on. Oh, I know the form, don't worry. I've had this kind of thing before. But you won't finish today, let me tell you that. I'm warning you. I've been doing this for years and you haven't. But it's your own doing." He was depressed by what he had done, by agreeing to this idiocy, but he had had to do it, he had had no choice. But now it was on, it was started, and he would die before he would give in.

"I'm enjoying myself, Gill," Muller said. "I always like to see what I can do. I'm like you. Only now we can see what both of us can do."

"You've got a touch of the sun, Muller."

"Yeah? And how about you? You've been crazy for years and you know it too."

"Huh. Save your breath, you're going to need it in a few hours." There was this bizarre intimacy, this hateful friendship struggling among their many antagonisms. Gilligan was worrying about it again.

They walked on, deeper and deeper into the wilderness. They could hear the Africans behind them bickering sleepily. Gilligan had always envied the Africans the way they switched on a kind of deep death when they went to sleep. Nothing kept them awake. They seemed to have no struggle with the things Europeans called "nerves" and "tension." They died and woke up again. He could hear that bastard, Jama, shouting the odds in his high, ranting Somali voice. How would Jama do today? It would be nice to walk a Somali down, and Gilligan felt he could do it.

20

THE SUN CAME UP, as always in this wilderness, like a raving giant in flames who had had to wait below the earth in darkness and impatience until he could come again and burn above for one more day of majesty. The tiny men stumbling on the great plain felt as if the sun had come up only for them, only to glare down on them. When they came to the first of the long high ridges which rolled like waves in a gradual ascent to the far forests, the sweat came out of them and soaked their khaki drill.

They were in form now, climbing in silence, their wills brooding in the agreement they had come to with their bodies. The sense of having engaged in something quite unnecessary was gone, and they had lost their stiffness and were full of new confidence.

Gilligan took longer, slower strides than Muller and never altered his pace, never gave his shoulder too much hope by moving the heavy rifle from it when it felt it could bear no more. For years and years Gilligan had done these lonely marches, and there was a special place in his person in which he could live in a thoughtful isolation, just as soldiers do under their burdens on the march. He carried on various dialogues in his skull, the mind forgetting the load of complaining flesh which it carried, as if the spirit had taken a second wind many years ago and could only be pulled down by a total exhaustion of the flesh, by death. Yesterday had been a kind of practice run for Gilligan. True he had overdone it, but today the body was obedient, almost quietly thrilled to know that it would be going on when Muller could go no farther.

Jama came running up, hawk-faced, trotting beside Gilligan, addressing him directly for the first time since the new agreement in the village by the river.

"What do *you* want?" Gilligan asked him without pausing.

"When do we have food? Nobody has had breakfast," Jama began.

"Bwana!" Gilligan shouted without turning his head, getting it in at once, this warning. He knew how Jama tried to ration that meaningful word out, tried to say it as seldom as possible.

"Bwana," said Jama, knowing what Gilligan felt. "When can we have a meal? The men want to know."

"*You* want to know, that's it, isn't it? None of the others would dare to ask such a question. They rely on the Bwana, that's why. When the Bwana eats they eat too. Why? Are you feeling weak? I thought you Somalis could go for days without food."

"When we have to we can go for a week," Jama said,

pricked by Gilligan's sharp needle. "But it is not like that now. We have eaten nothing today. Not even tea. I am dragged out of my blanket and told we are moving. I have had barely time to say my prayers—"

"When the Bwana eats you can eat too. Today you can show the others what you can do. And here's another thing, Jama. I am the master here. Do you hear? Now get back and be a Somali and don't come up here annoying me any more."

"Can we not even have tea?"

"Ask the other Bwana," said Gilligan, suddenly inspired. "Ask him if he will stop so that you can have tea. Try your English out on him." He looked at Muller. "A request from the oppressed masses," he said. "An appeal to your democracy."

"Yeah?" Muller smiled uncertainly. Jama went over to him and made his request.

"Men want have some tea, Bwana," Jama said. "Bwana Gilligan say up to you for men have tea. You let men have tea?"

"Bwana Gilligan said?" Muller flashed a look at Gilligan, who was grinning at him. "You want to stop?" Muller asked him.

"Me? I'm all right. This is your idea, this march. It's all yours, the decision. I've been the oppressor up to now, standing on the necks of Africa. But you see the way it gets you, Muller? You forget about democracy. You drive everyone out of the camp, none of them has had anything to drink yet, and now you can be a Senator and hear the voice of suffering Africa. You tell Jama the score. Tell him he can't have any tea because the two

Bwanas are busy. Tell him you want to show Bwana Gilligan who's really the best man, and there's no time for tea. Go on. Tell him. He's demanding his rights. He wants his tea."

"So you're loading it onto me, eh?" Muller's eyes glittered.

"You mean it's up to me whether they have their tea or not?"

"Work it out, chum," said Gilligan.

"Listen, Jama," Muller said, looking doubtful. "You'll just have to take it, see? The Bwana and me are having a competition. See? That means every guy here has to pitch in and do his stuff. That means you. See? We're not stopping for anything. We're making camp tonight. Now I don't have to tell a guy like you how to make out, do I? You get it? I'm not your master any more. You went back to Bwana Gilligan—" an edge came into his voice. "If you were still working for me I'd think about it. But if you've got a kick you'll have to tell your Bwana, Gilligan. Like I said, I don't want any tea. That's the way it goes. See?" But Jama began to argue. Gilligan listened and said nothing.

"Much troubles in this camp, Bwana," Jama said with the intensive delivery of his people when moving into an area of argument. "Men all unhappy. Why we have no tea?"

"Get back to your line," Gilligan said, and as Jama, incensed, began to declaim, Gilligan raised his voice until it overcame Jama's. "Get back and march. There's no tea. That's the order. *Amri yangu.* Tonight you can fill your belly but until then you march. There's no tea. And that's final. Now get back and don't let me hear another word out of you." He met Jama's fierce black eyes, and Jama dropped back, staring accusingly at Muller.

"That's the way it is, pal," Muller called to Jama weakly, feeling that somehow Gilligan, in a European way, had got him involved in a dirty European deal and had made him look like a Gilligan. A smart guy, Gilligan, passing the buck, sending Jama to him like that for a decision. All Muller had to do was say, "O.K. We'll have tea," and then Gilligan could have a rest, a rest called for by Muller. No damn fear. He knew how Gilligan's mind worked. He looked at Gilligan.

"I'm a smart guy too, Gill," he said. "You nearly had me there for a minute, didn't you?" He laughed. "But Jama's your man again. Me? I'm just the passenger, on trial, and this isn't my doing. You started this competition—"

"There's no competition, Muller. It's all in your head."

"In your hat," Muller said curtly.

"What's that mean?"

"Forget it."

"I told you this business was ridiculous. You force this thing on everybody and I have to be the cruel Bwana and oppress the natives so that you can be a hero. All right. I don't want an argument. I've had enough."

"But you think these guys should have their tea? I mean I don't want them to suffer—"

"You want to stop?" Gilligan eyed him keenly.

"I never said anything about stopping—"

"All right. Then let's forget it."

The ridges were becoming steeper, reminding Gilligan of those heartbreaking waves of ridges in Arakan in

Burma, ridges which threatened to stretch to the end of
the earth, one after the other. He got back into his hyp-
nosis, into his dream which separated mind and muscle,
Muller forgotten again.

Midday came like an unbearable load of flame pressing
down on the skull, burning through the khaki felt of their
stained bush hats. The sun searched inside their bodies,
seeking a corner where something would whimper. The
sun was right overhead, a gigantic blinding ball of flame
in a dry looking powdery-blue sky; the sky about the
sun looked like burned lime, whitish, powdery blue. The
earth seemed stunned, the twisted writhing thorn trees
stilled, a world for vultures, a kind of suburb of hell.

The two men drank from their water bottles as they
walked, not even having come to an agreement to stop for
a drink.

"Your elephant certainly has plenty of country to play
in," said Muller as they went down a ridge in a sliding
rattling cloud of stones.

"Yes, when you come into this country there's no end.
You can walk forever and there's no end. I love it. No
one will ever come here and build their bloody cinemas
and restaurants. It's too hot, too anti-softness, chum. No,
they'll never ruin this place with their lousy culture. It's
ruined already, ruined the way I like it, not their way.
You can die here and no bastard would ever know. The
tribes up here can live on nothing. They have to. You
get sorted out up here. This is like the world used to be
once, a place where the fit ones get the meat. That's the
real world, chum, no matter what you put on top of it
with cinemas and offices. Like it?" He grinned at Muller
and his sweaty face was hot and showed no tiredness. His

legs moved like slow brown pistons, his hard bare feet in the Somali sandals impervious to the prick of the small stones and shale which flowed through their open toes.

"Like it? You're not kidding when you say it's a place to sort guys out." Muller looked at Gilligan with a new interest, as if understanding a little more of him. "This has been your life, this kind of stuff? You never get tired of it? Never feel you've had enough?"

"When you're back in America, chum, among the ant-men again, you'll wish you were back here." He smiled. "You won't carry on this kind of caper if you come back here. You can't do this all the time, you know, what you're trying to do today. You go slow, a piece at a time, and you last out. Yes, I'll leave my bones in Africa, under some rock or other, and the bloody hyenas can eat me and that's that. I'd sooner have that than be buried in some churchyard among rows of others. I've had the good times and I have no complaints. Feeling all right?"

"I'm feeling *all right*," said Muller. "I'm feeling fine." But the sun had got into him and had wrecked some of the early morning's granite decision, taken the sweat out of his will. His head was aching. Even under the wide brim of the bush hat the sun stuck its white glaring swords into his mind. He wished he had dark glasses. Gilligan said he never wore them because you got to rely on them, and one day you lost them or broke them, and there you were with your eyes screaming for their crutches. No. Let the body take it, or else take it away and go in for market gardening outside of Nairobi or Arusha.

Midday seemed to last all afternoon in a stifling blanket of glaring heat. When he felt the cloth of his shirt

Muller could feel the dry heat in it. The sweat which came through the cloth was drunk up in one swift burning lick of the sun, leaving a thin white stain of salt, the body's real fuel. As the afternoon wore on, voices began in Muller's ear, and in Gilligan's. Muller's ear heard, 'He was right. It's ridiculous, this. Ridiculous. And yet it's great. No kidding, it's great. Here we are, two guys giving everything to an idea, endurance. It's ridiculous because it hurts, but it's great, actually. If you can go through to the end, that is. It's not great if you fall down. All that crap about trying is great too, even if you fail. No, Buster. What's great is trying and winning as well. So it's not really ridiculous. What's great about it is that it's for nothing, there's no prize and no medal. It's useless and we're doing it and it's great. Two men—' but all this quailed and retreated before the heat and before the growing onslaughts from his protesting muscles, and he fought back and started the voices again '—because whatever anyone says a guy has muscles, he's a man with qualities, of courage and toughness, and let's see what you've really got down there now the chips are down. Oh, they're down all right. Don't kid yourself. But it's useless. I mean do we have to do it?' Yes. Yes. Yes.

Gilligan was listening to an elephant talking, which was a part of himself, undiscovered territory, for he knew best what he had killed and mastered, the brash lion with tail straightened, a bundle of springing menace hit in midair between the eyes and stopped, then skinned, then forgotten, hundreds of times. Or the buffalo, his favorite frightener, mastered again, and again, hundreds of times, sometimes perilously, more terrible in many ways in thick bush, if mishandled, than the elephant, yet it was the elephant, of all the beasts, which had awaited him and which he had protected from all harm from himself ever since that night in the early days of his Africa when he had run. He would never run again. He was alone, actually. Muller was only here by accident, a stranger, paying for this trip, for him, Gilligan, to shoot himself. He almost stopped then in his long unknowing strides, saying those words again, 'to shoot himself,' for in a way that was what it really was, the journey to a slaying of the only part of himself he had imprisoned, where fear was. But why had there been that fear? Why should it be that what a man ran from was the thing he should rush at immediately afterward, like those pilots one read about who crashed their aircraft and had to go up again at once in another so as to retain mastery, not of the air, but of themselves. No? But yes.

It mattered. It had always mattered. Now, though, walking step by step toward this elephant, he was no longer able to shape the menace down to a seeable and faceable size. It was all about *then*, and now, about something so stupid that he could not understand why he had built this set of false walls around what he feared. He *would* kill the elephant. He would not let Muller kill it. Muller was a passenger on something much bigger than a hot walk after a trophy. He had never spoken to a single soul about his huge secret, his terror of elephants, for he had no right to this terror, a man without fear, known for so many narrow escapes before so many other much more dangerous beasts. He ought never to have allowed all this to come about, to have dodged this ceremony, for that was what it was, a ceremony, a ghost-banishing. 'Faster. Faster': this word rang in his skull during all the other cascades of ideas, visions, thoughts. In this kind of condition he could march forever, and yet, today, he knew he was injuring himself, was using up parts of himself too soon, too lavishly, and he would pay; because this was no ordinary safari, this was a kind of private pilgrimage. He felt as if he could do anything. He was screwing himself up for the occupation of the last unexplored area of his self, his laying of the ghost of that nonsensical mania, fear. And he knew he had never conquered fear, and had saved it up, secretly, all about elephants. How fantastic. How puerile. He wiped the sweat out of his eyes, feeling the bite of his own salt on his aching eyeballs.

Five o'clock on his sweat-wet wrist watch, the black soggy strap of which was trying to cool on his hot wrist. The sun like a huge bursting bomb above the blue-green mountains already quivering in night mist, the red twisting flames of the sun's coming death flaring and winding among the breaking shapes of the hastening dusk. He felt as if he was half out of his mind, and knew he was ready to stumble in coming fatigue. He looked at Muller, who was pale and set-faced, all jaw and clamped mouth, marching along in this senseless ceremony of boy scout manhood testing itself to the full, for nothing, and everything.

They had both survived the glaring torture of the day and already the first thin warm breezes were coming up, as if released from the sun's tyranny, cool on the face and sweaty neck, cold on the belly where they got through the opened shirt onto the soaking undershirt. Mad. Mad. But splendid. He was proud of Muller, in a way, in a hateful and grudging way, now they had seen the worst of the sun, but they were still far from that camp he could remember. 'All you have to do is be a man, courageous, and stop and say, "O.K. Muller, let's call it a day. It was great. Now let's grow up." ' *That* was courage, to say that and not care, not this stumbling on in weariness rather than not. No. Push that aside. On. On. On. Muller would go down eventually. He could not keep this up. He would go down. 'Down, you bastard. Down. Give up and who cares? I do.'

"What the hell are *you* laughing at?" Muller shouted, fierce and grim in his sweat.

"Was I laughing?"

'He's cracking,' Muller thought. 'He's tired out. He doesn't know he's laughing like a goddam loon.' But they went on, a few yards apart.

The Africans were spread out across the country behind them under their bundles, like a scene from eighteen ninety in darkest Africa, Jama in front, tireless, angry, vengeful.

21

IT WAS WHEN HE SAW the red winking of Chongu's fire
in the far distance that Muller's will began to collapse,
as if the fist clenched behind his solar plexus all this
while, and holding all the wires taut, had unclenched and
let everything go slack, so that he fell about on his feet
and spoke gibberish to himself aloud. He could hear
Gilligan's sandals a little ahead in the darkness, striding.
And Gilligan had heard Muller stumbling and had picked
up fleshly relish from that sign, and he had hastened his
pace, and he heard Muller hurrying after him, panting,
panting like a slavering animal.

'All in, you bastard,' Gilligan's self was yelling. 'All in.
All in. Done. Finished.' Both of them. Then he heard
Muller fall down, and he should have gone back, but he
didn't, couldn't; none of that nonsense about sportsmanship, not now at the end, not after this delirious ordeal
they had made for each other, separately, together in

clash, apart in reasons for the same thing, a victory. That fire of Chongu's must be about five to seven miles; ten times as big as a cigarette end in this thick warm sweating darkness, yes, it would be about seven million miles away. On. On. 'You're down, you bastard. Hard lines too. But down. It's all right, chum. Down. It's all right. Been down myself, for years, down now, and going up soon, to the finals, personal, you know. Never mind. You were good. You wanted the lot, and you were good. I'm good too. Better. The bloody best in fact. Best. On. Bash on regardless, chum. On.'

His body was operating without mind now, a succession of jerking and pushing movements, the mind sitting on the skull, gone, chattering like children. On.

Muller was up. Gilligan could hear him panting along behind—murmuring, muttering, drawing his breath in through his open, helpless mouth.

"You fell down, Muller," Gilligan shouted in a warning, hysterical voice. "Don't try it on, chum. I heard you. I bloody well heard you fall down. Heard you." And Muller could not keep up. He heard his panting falling behind. 'I'm done. Done. Can't make it,' Gilligan's voices were saying, and he let them become one, aloud, in a chant, "Faster. Faster. Faster. On. Press on, Jack. You've bust yourself, chum. You'll die for this. On." There was a knife of pain working its blade through his right knee, and another sawing through his right hip, and he knew that if he stopped, or fell down, he would never get up again and go on. Never. So on. On. Then, like a light going out slowly in his skull, he felt all the controls slipping from him, but he was moving, the body was going forward and nothing would stop it. But his command had gone and Chongu could hear him shouting and laughing from where he stood beside the fire up on the hill.

He was on his knees, not knowing how he had got there, and then fell forward on his hands, his rifle slipping slowly on its sling from his shoulder. He was going to fall down on his face, gladly, but he could not do it. Waves of terrible relief were flowing up through his body from his feet, accompanied by surges of pain and weakness. Up. Up. He heard feet coming, did not want to be seen down, pressed himself up with a great effort by using his hands as two springs, so that he was kneeling again; got one leg lifted, picked up the rifle and held it as a crutch, began to drag himself up by the rifle as Muller stumbled up in the moonlight. Muller's panting was so loud that Gilligan looked up at him, groaning in exertion as he got to his feet. He smiled tiredly. Muller looked as if he was right out of his mind, eyes staring, white-faced, and glistening with sweat. He took one look at Gilligan and reeled forward again.

"You went down, Muller," Gilligan cried, accusingly, wanting it on record, wanting it known that he knew, and Muller turned and gasped, "So were you. Saw you. Quits. It's on again." Then he turned and reeled forward again. Gilligan was gathering everything up now, pulling the rifle up onto his shoulder, taking unrelenting command of the imploring flesh once more, and then he launched it forward again, nearly falling before his weary legs could catch up with the impetus he had given himself. He drew up with Muller. He was laughing so loud that it echoed on the dark African plain, and Muller looked at him with his staring eyes, puzzled, only half understanding, not really in touch any more.

"Funny?" was all he could get out.

"What's funny?" Gilligan said hoarsely. Then he raised his voice in complaint, saying, "You shouldn't have done this, you bastard. I shouldn't have let you do it." He was referring to physical fears which this ordeal had aroused in his body, for he knew he had damaged it, had hastened what could have waited and been spread out over years, and he could feel this in every muscle, that he had given himself a deadly blow today. For the first time he had felt age and had lashed it away, driving the apparatus on until its bitter complaints and warnings had been engulfed by the fantasy of his will. He felt that when he lay down he would never rise again. He was fifty-seven at last, and he felt very much older, and querulously fearful now that the mad day was done and he could see that fire winking on the hill.

Muller did not reply to his accusing shouts. He was all in, hardly able to handle half a sentence that passed into his ears before it evaporated in his immense struggle to go on and win, and Gilligan had passed him. He could not catch up with Gilligan and he knew it, and all he could hope for was that Gilligan would fall down again when they came to that last hill on which Chongu's fire burned.

Now Jama came moving up, carrying two rifles, one on each shoulder. Aganaza had fallen face down two hours ago, and the other Africans were lying on their backs and faces for miles back. Jama came up now in long, easy strides, his white turban glowing in the moonlight. He came up to Muller.

"You feel well, Bwana?" he asked.

"I'm all right I told you," Muller screamed. "Quit asking me, will you?" He fell away from Jama, not seeing him, caught control of his buckling legs again and straightened out, eyes fixed madly again on that fire on the hill.

Jama watched him closely, saw how far gone he was, and then paced after Gilligan whom he could hear mumbling and declaiming ahead. He caught up with him at the foot of the long slowly ascending hill.

"Give me your rifle, Bwana," he said, almost commanded, holding out his hand. "You and the other Bwana are tired out."

"Has the other Bwana got *his* rifle?" Gilligan cried through his teeth, his face dripping with sweat in the moonlight. "Eh? Eh?"

"Other Bwana has his rifle," Jama said.

"Then get back. Back," Gilligan shouted, falling about as he began the ascent of the hill. Jama's freshness was an insult to him and he did not want to see any more of it. He glared at Jama accusingly. "Go on. Back. Back."

"But Bwana, you look very ill. Give me your rifle and I will get the other Bwana's rifle," Jama pleaded with him. Gilligan's gasps and pantings were like those of a man in terrible pain.

"Back, I said," Gilligan yelled, his voice crackling. "Back." He charged at the hill and went falling up it, steadying himself as his tottering feet made their last effort.

Cursing in a whisper in his own tongue, Jama went up the hill like a gazelle, passing Gilligan, noiselessly, out of hearing, he thought. He was carrying a kettle, tea, and condensed milk and sugar, and two enamel mugs he had taken from Aganaza's load. He went up the hill so fast that Gilligan, who was shaking his fist at him and trying to threaten, lost sight of him after a few seconds.

Half an hour later Chongu saw Gilligan falling into the camp, the rifle dropping from his shoulder. Like somebody dying and seeking a place for himself away from other men, he went staggering past the fire and then pitched onto his face, unconscious.

Jama, tending the kettle, worriedly looked at Chongu and said, "You see? I told you. They have driven each other since before dawn this morning, and this one has won, and look at him." Chongu burst out laughing, pressing his hand over his mouth to silence himself, and Jama grinned up at him. "Anyway," he said to Chongu, "they are men, not like these slaves. The slaves fell down, whimpering. Even the great Aganaza, whom Bwana Gilligan thinks so much of, fell crying like a woman into the grass. Give this tea to the Bwana. If he is alive." They laughed all over again at this and Chongu went over to Gilligan with the mug of tea, but Gilligan was far beyond tea. Chongu turned him over and held his head and poured the tea into his mouth, tasting it first to test its heat. It went down Gilligan's throat but he did not open his eyes. Chongu was alarmed, for he was deeply attached to Gilligan.

Then Muller appeared in the wide flicker of the firelight, tears on his face. He went down where he paused to stand, on his haunches, meaning to sit, but fell slowly onto his back, finished, his rifle still on his shoulder. Jama and Chongu grinned at each other.

"Give him tea," said Jama.

"My Bwana won," Chongu said, looking down admiringly at Gilligan.

"No. *I* won," Jama said. "I won."

"It is not the same thing," Chongu replied. "A black man is bound to win in the end against white men. We are in our own land. But that does not count. I am talking about the white men. Mine won."

"*I* won." Jama jumped to his feet, his fist pressed on his chest. "Now give the other one his tea. Then go and find the others, the slaves, or there will be some real trouble when these two fools wake up and want their food and their beds, and the rest of it."

"Yes," Chongu nodded, remembering that efficiency and the things of the camp came first. He called Gavai. "Come on, old fellow," he said. "We have work to do."

22

THE NEXT DAY TAXED JAMA to the full, for he had to take command of the whole distorted situation, with Gilligan unconscious and delirious, and Muller lying prone and speechless in the shade of a thorn tree. Reports carried by Gavai came back occasionally from Chongu. Aganaza was only able to hobble a little way at a time. Some of the other men were fitter and were carrying the kit in.

"Get the medicine," Jama said, seizing Gavai by the throat. "I told you to bring the medicine and the drink, didn't I?" He shook the little frightened hunter. "I told you it is in a red box. Get it, and if you come here again without it I'll kill you. Medicine and drink. Get it from Aganaza. Now go."

He was nursing Gilligan and Muller, bathing their foreheads with cold compresses, bringing them tea. It looked as if Gilligan was dying. Once Gilligan had opened fierce, hot blue eyes, stared ferociously at Jama, and shouted,

"Back. Back. Get Back," and then began to babble in English and Ki-Swahili. Muller was quite silent, as if in a deep drugged sleep, unmoving, white-faced, and looking much thinner than he had yesterday.

It was late afternoon when Jama had all the kit in the camp, and all the Africans had trailed in, their morale gone. Aganaza crawled, weeping softly, into a patch of grass and lay there like a battle-exhaustion case, wanting to be forgotten for a while, but Jama rooted him out and gave him work to do. This helped Aganaza, though he showed his resentment at Jama's having taken over the running of the camp. Jama gave military-type orders, lining everyone up and allotting tasks, slapping men on the face if they dawdled or tried to creep away for a little rest somewhere.

Two hours after darkness came down, Muller got up from his place under the tree and hobbled over to the fire where Jama was cooking a meal. He sat down beside Jama and stared into the fire with dazed eyes.

"What happened, Jama?" he asked. "I been asleep long?" Having made as casual a job as possible of those questions, to which he did not want a reply, he went on, looking at Jama, "Who won? Who came in first?"

"I come first," Jama said, smiling, his long white teeth flashing in his well-cut bluish-black lips. "Jama first. Somali mans longest walker, strong mans."

"I'm not talking about Somali mans," Muller said angrily, provoked by Jama's smiling self-satisfaction. "I'm talking about Bwana Gilligan and me. Who won?"

"Bwana Gilligan number two," said Jama solemnly, nodding, his lips compressed. "Bwana Gilligan second mans."

"Yeah?" Muller gripped his arm and shook it, half rising. "So I made it. I made it. You saw me come in first? Huh?"

"Jama first," came the correction. "Then Bwana Gilligan number two. Then you, Bwana."

Muller collapsed onto his haunches again, sank his head into his arms, and uttered a long, moaning sigh of despair. He looked so tragic that Jama, with the quick Somali way of knowing which white man would take what, did something he would never have thought of doing with Gilligan. He put his hand on Muller's shoulder and patted it, laughing hoarsely, saying, "You strong mans, number three. Bwana Gilligan he number two, fall down in grass like dead mans. You fall over there." He pointed beyond the fire. "Jama come first, make tea ready for you. You sleep all day like dead mans. Bwana Gilligan very sick. Say nothing but shouts. Very sick mans. You give him whisky, Bwana, that make him strong mans again." Muller sat on with his head on his arms.

23

GILLIGAN DID NOT COME OUT of his delirium for nearly forty-eight hours, and by then Jama had organized the camp and Aganaza was able to walk about again.

It was an agony for Gilligan to see Muller walking about, as if nothing had happened, no terrific ordeal undergone. There was a dark, oily, bitter taste in Gilligan's throat which he recognized, the bile taste of old malarias dragged up out of the physical upheaval he had forced on himself. He lay weak and dreamy, looking up at the blue sky through the lacework of the thorn canopy above him. He knew he had won. No matter how Muller waltzed around the camp he had not won, and for the first time in his life Gilligan lay back on his age and felt proud with what he had done. 'I'm fifty-seven and I beat him. That shows you, you see, all this bloody talk and bull. Fifty-seven and I beat him.' He called for Aganaza. Nearly everyone in the camp came with him to where Gilligan lay.

"Aganaza, not *you* lot," Gilligan said, forcing his weak voice into commanding sound. "This isn't the bloody hospital, you know. Clear off and get on with your work." Smiling, nudging each other, the Africans drifted away, saying, "He's well again. He's angry."

"How are you feeling Bwana?" Aganaza asked. His eyes were full of amusing self-pity, for he wanted Gilligan to know what a torment he had been put through on that march.

"Are you going to cry all over me or something, Aganaza?" Gilligan said, severe and pitiless. "Don't. I'm too busy for it. What I want to know is, Who was first? It was me, wasn't it?"

"You came first," Aganaza said. "You have been very sick. You are not young now. You should not do these things with young men like the other Bwana."

"That's impudent," Gilligan said. "Don't be impudent to me, Aganaza. I won, didn't I? That's all that matters. What news of the elephant? Has Chongu done anything or has he been wasting his time here? I want a full report."

Aganaza told of how Chongu had taken on a man called Gavai as tracker, a man who knew where the elephant was. Yes, it was still alive and, Bwana, as dangerous as ever. Muller came up and Gilligan dismissed Aganaza. The two white men stared at each other.

"Hard lines, pal," said Muller. "But for a man of your age you were pretty good. I don't mind admitting to you that I was dying after sunset on that walk. Never mind, it was all worth it. Hard lines on you."

"What are you getting at now, Muller?" Gilligan said in a low voice. "Hard lines about what? I'm all right. I'm resting, that's all. First rest I've had in twenty years and

I'm enjoying it too. So cut the hard lines stuff, please."

"I'm not talking about your lying on your back and taking it easy," Muller said. "You're finished. I know that. Who can kick about that at fifty-seven? You did well, pal. But we weren't up to Jama's standard. I've no hard feelings, have you? That guy can sure step it out." He laughed, shaking his head in admiration of Jama. "Not only walked in first but had tea ready for us two wrecks. Well, hard lines, pal."

"Now listen to me, Muller," Gilligan's eyes almost closed. He got up on his right elbow and pointed a finger at Muller. "Don't you start that one with me. I won't have it, chum. I was in to this bloody camp first, chum, and don't you forget it. Don't you try and bend it into something else. *I* was first."

"Jama was first," said Muller. "He walked us both into the ground."

"I won't have that. I won't have it." Gilligan hammered the side of the camp bed, looking old and gray-grizzled with his three days of stubble as he stared up at Muller. "Cut it out. I'm not going to allow that one. Are you trying to tell me that it was Jama who was first and not me? I'm talking about US, chum. You and me. Jama doesn't count. I don't go in for contests with Africans. And neither did you until I beat you. So cut out this new bull. You lost. And I won."

"If that's your attitude to sportsmanship, then O.K." Muller looked offended, on his dignity. "We'll leave it there, then. Jama's a black. Fine. Blacks can't win. Right. Let's leave it like that."

"You save that for a speech somewhere about democracy." Gilligan was so excited he almost forgot his pains.

"You won't fool anybody with that, Muller. I won. And you lost." He watched Muller turn on his heel and walk away. He smiled after him, licking his lower lip. "I WON, CHUM," he shouted. "Not Jama. But me. Me." Then he lay down again and lit a cigarette.

III. The Elephant

24

THE OLD BULL LIKED TO WANDER early in the cool morn-
ings. There was a large lump of lead in his body, near
his great left hipbone; it had lain there since long before
the first white men had come into eastern Africa. It had
been fired into him by an Arab one peaceful, silent
morning, suddenly, with a clap of thunder to go with it,
and he had been running away ever since, from a peculiar
smell, and from unusual sounds. In the early morning the
deep ache in his hip seemed to lessen, and his appetite
felt good and sharp then. He did not like the heat. He
was very touchy and particular.

Ages had passed since he had first joined the big herds
in forests far from here, and it had been a world of silence
then.

In that time ages ago the world had belonged to the
beasts, and to the Africans who had fed on them, men
who had had to train to hunt, who had gone through

rituals and had pitted themselves against real danger in the hunt for meat. Men had not slain them then for their tusks so much as for their meat when hungry.

The great herds were gone now, vanished with the fusillades and the sounds of chopping knives cutting out the big tusks which had had ages in which to grow to heavy, yellow maturity. And then the new men began to shoot the young and retreat again, a departure before civilization.

It was hundreds of miles from here, where he grazed now, that the old bull's early life had been spent, in a country cooler and richer than this one he hid in now. Not far away from where he stood with his slowly waving trunk was his companion, a young bull who would stay with him in an understood commitment until he died. This young bull was spry and watchful, always ahead, always watching and sniffing and suspicious, as mad in his way as his ancient friend. Their life together in the huge silence had made a bond of understanding between them. They were far from the herd with which the old bull had finished his affairs years ago. One day the young bull would rejoin the herd, alone, his duty done and an old and tested friendship finished.

Sometimes they went together on long journeys to the river, far up from the villages where it did not stink of men, and there crunch up *dom* nuts and go wild with appetite among luscious foliage, but the old bull had made fewer and fewer of these journeys in the last year or two. He was not as fast as he used to be, and was bad-tempered and did not like to be led too far by the younger, adventurous one.

They had come from the wallow and were shining with

soft red mud, the yellow sunlight winking and glittering on it as they meandered back into the trees. It was silent and hot and the air was full of the scent of rank white blossom among the thorns. They stood for a while, listening, quite still, drops of mud rolling on their thick leather and falling in steam to the warm red sand they stood in. All well. They moved on, lazily, tearing down a morsel here, smashing a tree there, two obsolescent giants going back into hiding so as to live for a little longer.

The old bull was carrying huge ivory, curios of his race which had vanished many fusillades ago, into game books, into billiard balls, into Chinese carvings and Indian inlaid tables, into cash from Mombasa to Hong Kong and to Berlin. The old elephant hunters, who had had the best of it at a time when Gilligan was young, would stand and pick their bulls as the herds stampeded, killing one right then left until the herd milled and they could shoot as they chose. Some of them killed forty and fifty at a time, trails of enormous skeletons like beached ships lying in their wake. Long chanting troops of Africans, tusks resting on their heads, had marched from the great lakes behind the bearded malarial Bwanas to the ivory markets on the coast. And all that was done with now, something for research in colleges, the memoir of a savage appetite.

The two bulls moved deeper into the thick, high scrub, secure, and fearless. A dozing rhinoceros, startled by the screeching tickbirds which had lifted in alarm from his back, panicked and went charging blindly through the thorns. A sleeping leopard some distance away rose silently, crouching, dusty gold-and-black fur glowing in the sunlight, yawned, and then padded silently to somewhere quieter. The slow steady crash of the elephants aroused the sleepers of the hot afternoon, sending them to deeper places in the thickets.

Gavai came out of the trees on his toes, crouching, listening, his eyes wide in his pauses, head turning right and left before he moved on in his skillful silence. Chongu was a few yards behind him, taller, longer of leg, a Nilotic with flared nostrils and proud sullen lips, red ocher plastered on his knotted hair. Gavai carried a bow, a quiver of long freshly poisoned arrows lashed to his left shoulder with rawhide cords. Chongu held a long spear which rested gently on his slender right shoulder.

Gavai would stop, trembling all over as his small hard black eyes studied the sign in the sand, and behind him Chongu would wait until Gavai turned his head and pointed with his hand, when both would move on again. It was not till late evening that they came on the first new dung of the elephant, great squarish blocks like compressed steaming shredded tobacco, fearless dung of beasts with no apprehensions that they were being followed. Long blue broken shadows were falling across the hot sand now, and the blue misty silence of night was welling up from the hollows in the bush. In the silence the two hunters could hear the sweet ripple of water not far off. Gavai looked at Chongu, pointing with his chin, and Chongu agreed with his lips, and they loped off together toward the water.

They squatted down by it, picking it up cold in their hands and pouring it down their dry throats. Chongu took two cold baked potatoes out of his satchel and offered one to Gavai, who refused it, saying he never ate potatoes because they constipated him. He had a lot to say against the potato, affirming his faith in maize and meat, so Chongu ate the potatoes, one in each hand. Chongu's favorite food was a can of corned beef soused with the hot brown watery sauce of which Bwana Gilligan always had several bottles in his chop-box, but it was hard to get at them with Aganaza always on the prowl.

Gavai took a blackish coil of dried meat from around his neck, put the end in his mouth, and then sliced pieces of it off with his dagger, like an Abyssinian.

"The elephants are farther off than they were," he told Chongu. "And they are moving away all the time. It has taken me a day more to reach them this time than it did last time. They are moving away all the time."

"I will go back for the white men," said Chongu. He laughed. "They are both weary after their anger with each other, after all their walking. They are strong, and stupid together. My Bwana is not like that when he is alone, but since this new white man joined him he is not himself. One cannot speak with him in case he strikes out. This is a bad safari."

"I never worked for a white man and I never will," said Gavai. "I have never had much to do with them and I hate the smell they have, and I cannot understand what they say to me. I am no good for that work."

"You have your smell too, old fellow. I can smell you here now."

"I can smell you too," said Gavai, sniffing the air, "but the white smell is like a cat mixed with a dead thing. It is a strange smell."

"It is their soap and their sweat," Chongu told him. "Their sweat is different from ours, and their soap makes it worse. But you get used to it. A good white man is a good thing. You have to know your white man, like I know mine. Mine is mad, they say, but I never found him mad. I do my work and he is satisfied."

"Do you ever get your hands on his bottles?" Gavai asked, looking keenly at Chongu. "Has he got many bottles with him?"

"There are bottles, but I never drink from them. I drank some of the stuff once. It was far from here when I was a stupid youth. I went out of my mind with it in a town and was in great trouble, ending in a jail. I have never drunk from one of their bottles since then. I'll get you one of the bottles when all is over and the elephant is dead."

"Good. When will you call the white men? To-morrow?"

"Now," said Chongu, rising easily on one leg and hefting his spear.

"There are lions here. It is a long way."

"A lion is nothing to me, old fellow," Chongu smiled at Gavai. "Now keep your eyes on these elephants. I will bring the white men to this stream. They will camp here." He took the old man's arm gently, looking into his eyes, searching and warning him. "And remember, I know how you people forget and sometimes fail to keep your promises. Do not fail me and go away from here, for I will have to follow you and I will put this through you." He showed Gavai his spear. Gavai shook his head.

"I will be here," he said. "You will never have to hunt for me with your spear."

"Good. And then there is the tobacco. Always remember the tobacco that is waiting. Plenty of it."

"I have not forgotten it."

"Good." Chongu lifted his long spear onto his shoulder.

"And gather wood for the fire. Clear a camp site. And watch the elephants until we come for them. We will be here quickly."

Gavai watched Chongu loping down the trail through the thorns toward the plain, envying him his youth, his height, his casual and easy nobility of behavior. When Chongu had gone he went back to examine the elephant dung, making up a time picture of it and of the probable distance from here of the two elephants. As darkness poured down after the sunset, he went back to the stream to smoke a pipe and then to sleep.

25

THE REACTION HIT MULLER just as he thought he had recovered from the great march, just as he was about to spend some time at Gilligan's bedside, for Gilligan still lay on his back and was taking whisky and quinine as tonics. It was heatstroke which had affected Muller. He had to make his way to his bed holding onto trees, feeling his senses leaving him and an almost delicious weakness overcoming him. He talked nonsense to Jama who came to see him. Sweat was pouring from his body and he was white-faced, delicious. Aganaza carried the news to Gilligan, to whom it gave fresh life, and he actually pulled himself out of his bed and walked, stiff-legged and weakly to see Muller, but feeling better every minute.

He nursed Muller himself, wrapping him in a soaking cold sheet until his temperature came down, giving him well-salted water to drink, and eventually came the two great moments for him, one because Muller came to to see Gilligan nursing him, the victor helping the gallant loser, and the other moment for his own pleasure in seeing Muller well again, for he had grown angrily fond of the American. A poisoned intimacy had developed between them, and they had begun to understand each other's deficiencies, recognizing their own fearful devotion to physical manliness in each other, and seeing it as ridiculous, while knowing it was vital to them.

"I knew you'd overreached yourself, Muller," Gilligan said. He was sitting on a chop-box beside Muller's light steel-framed camp bed. "But I'll give you this. You're a sticker, the way you got onto your feet so soon, too soon actually. This is the reaction setting in now."

Muller looked into his eyes and smiled without opening his tight lips, shaking his head at this maddening incorrigibility. And then he threw his grenade into Gilligan's smugness, into that insufferable vanity. He had to, not only for his own sake, but for Gilligan's sake too, for it would not be long now until they were in front of the elephant. Chongu had come back to the camp with his tidings of the two elephants.

"Do you reckon you're going to get rid of your elephant fixation, Gill?" he said. "Because it won't be long now. I know you're pretty screwed up about the whole thing. How do you feel about it now? O.K.?"

He was taken aback by Gilligan's immediate reply. "Yes. I think I can face it this time," said Gilligan. He hid his shock. 'Elephant fixation,' he thought. 'Yes. Muller always knew.'

"You're a cool guy," Muller said, his wide watchful eyes fixed on Gilligan's. "Real cool." He was seized by a fit of laughing, still watching Gilligan's eyes.

"You're a man, Muller. I mean a Man. I wouldn't admit what I've just admitted to anyone but you. I'm not ashamed of it." He was so ashamed that he could hardly look into Muller's wary eyes.

"Yes, you are. You have to be ashamed," said Muller. "You can't afford that kind of thing with your record. All that stuff about loving elephants. That never fooled me. Being scared's no harm. Say, give me a whisky, will you, Gill. I feel like I've been dead for ten years." Gilligan called for Aganaza and whisky.

"I *want* to talk about it, Muller," Gilligan said, peering like an inquisitor into Muller's cautious eyes. "I'm not here just for the money, though I want that, I want that like hell. You say being scared is no harm. You're wrong there."

"I've been scared all my life," Muller began, but Gilligan waved his hand, frowning, saying, "I don't want to hear any of that. I don't want to hear about it. Don't try and console me. I don't need consoling. I've only ever been scared of one thing and that's an elephant, and I know why. I let it climb on top of me once, that's why. But I've taken risks that would have turned your hair gray. I'm not ashamed. I'm not a windy type, Muller. But I got myself messed up about elephants." His face changed, became racked, like a man being taken to the torture, as if he had let everything which haunted him rise out of its caves and show itself. "You don't know what I've gone through. You can't imagine what I've suffered with this thing, me, a man famous for guts, a fellow who's proved thousands of times that he fears nothing. Look—" He tore open his shirt and showed Muller long thin purple scars under his right armpit and along his ribs.

"Yeah, I've noticed those before," said Muller. "I settled for war wounds. Right?"

"Lion scars, chum. I smashed a lion down once on the Athi plains and while I was having a look over it the lioness came and put me down and started to have lunch off me, and I killed the bitch with my knife. I cut her bloody throat while she was trying to eat me. Now that takes guts, I don't care what you say. You mean to say that was the action of a windy man? You mean to say that someone who's done things I've done can be called windy because I've let myself get warped about elephants?" There was despair in his weary blue eyes.

"I've never called you windy, as you call it," Muller protested. Now that he was getting them, he did not want these revelations, but he knew he would ask for more. In other men lay every man's secrets.

"No, but you've thought it. I've listened to your insinuations and I know you've had your mind poisoned by gossip about me." Gilligan spoke bitterly, accusingly. "Don't bother denying it, it doesn't matter a bugger to me right now. But I'm telling you the facts. I'm clueing you up. I'm proud. I'm a proud man. All right. Why shouldn't I be? My record's second to none. Now here's what I want. You have a movie camera in your kit. I want you to film me shooting the elephant. I want it on record." He began to forget himself, to lose control of himself, snatching the glass of whisky from Aganaza, who had poured one also for Muller. "I've had to put up with years of backbiting, Muller. Years of it. And I've gone through it in my own mind. But this time I'm going to show you something. I'm going to let that elephant get right on to me before I smash it down, and I want it photographed, for all time. For all time. Chongu says there are two elephants. I want the young bull. It'll be a bull like the old one, they always operate that way. I'll show you who's windy." But he wanted the old bull as well. He put his hands to his face, sighing, dragging his big hands down his cheeks so that his eyes stood out. "It's the highest honor I could pay you, Muller, telling you a dirty secret like that. But in some ways you've measured up to what I call a man, and anyway you know that I've got more guts in my little finger than you have in your whole body, and I mean that as a compliment."

"I told you you were a screwball, Gill."

"I know you did. You wanted to start this American tinkering with my works and everything. I wouldn't let you, would I? Why? I'll tell you, chum. Because it's all bloody bunk, that's why, all this psycho stuff. A man has to do it himself, and if he can't do that, then he's no good. You wanted to start finding if my mother wouldn't give me a teddy bear when I was three so that I wanted to kill her for it or something. Don't look surprised. I may be a bush stiff in some ways but I can read, and I know bunk when I come across it. Things are simpler than that, you know. I don't need a trick cyclist to ride around in me to find out what's the matter, chum. I know what's the matter. I'm frightened of elephants. That's simple. My mother had nothing to do with that. *I* did that." He was tragic as he pressed his fists on his chest and looked beyond Muller, Muller forgotten.

"You can ruin your whole life by one moment's failure," Gilligan went on. "You can mark yourself for life by a sudden wrong decision. Another man, a weaker person, would have committed suicide after what I did, but you have to have guts to live and wait. And I've waited. How do we know if we're not ill, something wrong with us mentally and physically when we fail like I failed? Here's a man who went through the First World War, when war was war, chum, ten million shells *before* the worst part, going over the top. I was seventeen. I did all that and won a medal for bravery. I've shot all kinds of men and every kind of big game under all kinds of conditions. I served in the worst of the Burma campaign, got another medal, a better one that time, and I've done things that would have turned an ordinary man's hair gray. Why, then, have I let myself get a thing about an elephant? Why?"

"Mine's women," Muller said. "I can't fight a woman. I just fade instead. I get on the goddam airplane or the train and fade. I've been yellow too in other ways, like once when I pretended I was sick in the war. But I got up and went and did my stuff. I couldn't stay back. I had to go on being able to live with myself. But I knew I was through, even though—"

"Some years after I developed my elephant thing," Gilligan said, ignoring Muller's admissions, "I gave myself a real test. I went with some Masai and used a spear on a lion." Frantically he asked his question again. "I tell you I've done these things. Why, then, should I get messed up about an elephant?"

"How do you know you can face it now?" Muller asked.

"I don't know," Gilligan whispered, still looking far off. He got up and paced about, as if alone. "But I'll have to. I always knew I'd have to. And I've got to do it. There's no way out now. I've forced myself into the position. It's got to be done. There's no escape. I'll do it. I've got to. Have to do it. I'll do it. And I want it on record. I want it photographed." He turned and looked at Muller. "Keep your money, Muller, and let me shoot the old bull. You can have all of it, but let me kill the bastard."

"Wait till we get there," Muller said.

"You mean wait till I see how I'm feeling when we see the elephant?" Gilligan's voice was bitter and defensive.

"There are some things a guy just can't beat," Muller said. "Some things you just have to live with. Mine's women. I can't—"

"I don't want to hear about you and women, Muller. I've never shot a woman and I'm not likely to, even if one charged. This has got nothing to do with that kind of nonsense. I'm talking about courage, a man's courage. I've got all anyone could need, more than most, but I'm not able to—" He stopped, clenching his teeth in anguish "—I hope I'll never regret telling you what I've told you. I hope you realize what trust I've put in you. It's the highest compliment I could pay you."

"When do we start?"

"As soon as you're well."

"As soon as *I'm* well? How about you? You look like you could use a pair of crutches. You want to see yourself walking around like—"

"That'll do, thank you." He had forgotten to pretend that all was well with him. He had been limping about, even groaning, in sight of Muller. "I was bloody angry with you for trying that Jama thing on me, Muller, trying to make out that Jama was the winner. It was a fair contest and I won. But I don't mind telling you it's taken it out of me, but not as much as it's taken it out of you."

"O.K. O.K." Muller said, sighing exasperatedly, lying back on his bed. "O.K. I give in."

"If you're fit enough we'll start out tomorrow."

"I'll be fit enough," Muller said. "I'm no goddam invalid. A touch of the sun, that's all. There's no need to shout your head off about it." He wanted to be alone to think about Gilligan, about this revelation he had made, this handing over of himself with his secret. He did not like it, and he did not know why.

26

HE KNEW IT WAS PITY which had made him listen to Gilligan's confession, pity for himself as well. He had almost stopped him and said, "Don't go on. You'll regret this later. You'll hate me for knowing. I don't want to hear you unloading. You've kept it in the dark all these years, so don't tell *me* about it. I don't want to be hated for knowing." But pity had made him listen.

He felt no contempt for Gilligan, now that he knew. But they had grazed so much of each other's pride already, they had hurt each other so much in their contest—a contest which seemed to be organized from outside of both of them—that Gilligan's confession now felt like a burden to him. He felt afraid, now that he knew. The confession had made him a kind of prisoner of Gilligan.

'He's mad,' Muller found himself thinking on the march. 'And now he's told me everything can he ever say goodby? Can he ever let me go? A guy like this could

186

shoot you, now you've heard his confession.' He saw
Gilligan standing over his bed in the darkness, shooting
him; Gilligan dragging his body to a ravine and pushing
it over the edge, saying, "Now everything's the way it
used to be. It's all unsaid again," and then having a beer.
'I suppose that's what I'd do,' Muller thought. Yet the
new look in Gilligan's eyes was surely enough to dispel
such fears. A look of sadness and resignation had appeared
in Gilligan's eyes now, like the look you would expect
to find in the eyes of an old and weary man. He was still
full of his vain and spiky self, but there was a resignation
in his eyes which had been brought there by the load of
sudden age he had dragged down upon himself by that
terrible march, and the load had forced the confession.
He had begun to give up. He was becoming honest and
honesty was the worst policy for the dedicatedly brave
and combative, for those who lived in terror of fear. It
was Gilligan himself who spoke of these things as they
walked over the hot rocks toward the elephants, Muller
listening uneasily. He was getting too much of inner
Gilligan, too much surrender.

"This safari has done for me, Muller," he heard Gilligan saying. There was a kind of melancholy anger in his
voice. "I didn't let Pratt down so much as myself. I never
faced it aloud before. What's the worst thing *you*'ve
ever done?" He wanted Muller to be his companion in
some kind of guilt, if possible, and Muller knew it and
responded.

"O.K., I'll tell you the worst thing I ever did," he said
in a strange, cold voice, so that Gilligan glanced sharply
at him and Muller met his glance and smiled knowingly.
"I'm telling you this so you won't feel as much of a heel

as you do right now. Listen, for Christ's sake don't hate me because you've told me that about you and Pratt—"

"I'm not going to hate you for that, you bloody fool," Gilligan said harshly, "What do you think I am? A woman or something?" But there was hatred in his eyes when Muller looked into them.

"So I'll tell you," Muller said, raising his cold voice. "We're dishing the dirt and I'll give you a hand. I'll dive in with you because as sure as hell that's what you want, isn't it? I told you I didn't want to hear your goddam story but you told it. Now I'll tell you mine. And it's about what drives people like you and me crazy, and I mean about being one hundred per cent true to yourself all the time, about being—I mean about being a real man—"

"Ah, come to the bloody point," Gilligan snarled in an anguish of embarrassment. "Cut out the American bullshit. What do you want to *say*?"

They were well ahead of the Africans. Muller, screwed tight in emotion evoked by what he needed to say, and had never said, and did not quite understand, gripped Gilligan's arm while they walked, and shook it, crying, "Running away's not the worst thing you can do. Cut your limey inferiority crap about America and listen—"

"All *right*," Gilligan snapped at him, tearing his arm away from Muller's grasp. "Just stop the bloody drama, that's all, and let's have the story. I can't stand all this emotion. There's no bloody need for it."

Muller rolled his eyes up in mock and real rage, and said what he wanted to say, fiercely, as if Gilligan had forced him to say it, ranting it as if accusing Gilligan of what it all meant to him, Muller.

"I'm telling you about the greatest guy I ever knew, and I only knew him in the flesh for about two hours, but those two hours go on in my head all the time. And here's the pay-off. He was a Jap. A Jap colonel who asked me to do him a favor, and I forced the bastard to live instead. They're the bravest, the Japs. The bravest of the brave—"

"DON'T SAY THAT," Gilligan pushed the words out in a sort of agonized shout. "Those despicable bloody suicides, stupid slaves, you had to kill them all or they killed themselves, don't you try and sell me the Japs." Here was a disturbed area. Singapore. The Empire. The Little Yellow Men who had smashed it in Asia and who had shown that no one had anything to teach them about how to die, or how to be pitiless.

Muller smiled and slapped Gilligan on the back. "I know how you feel, pal. They made bravery as we know it look like combat neurosis. So I'll tell you." He raised his cold voice again and seemed to speak out of a long-closed icebox in which he had buried his unkowingly Christian sin, a sin smeared with the Christian gift of pity disguised as hatred and jealousy, and even as he spoke it he could not understand it. And he spoke of pity. "And Jeeze, did those guys hate pity! It really frightened them. But I hated that Jap colonel so much, for *everything*, that I wouldn't let him kill himself, and he was kneeling down, fit to be tied, begging me for a gun, a rope, any goddam thing so he could go through with his samurai routine. Get it? He was my prisoner and I would't let him do what he wanted most. Knock himself off. I made the bastard live. You know how it was with the Japs. Well, this colonel had commanded the three days of hell I

and my company had before we killed every single bastard
of them, and then got the colonel alive." His voice
trembled, rose. "Which was O.K. with them, of course,
dying, being killed, the bastards loved it, don't forget
that, they loved to die—"

"Don't tell *me*," Gilligan cut in. "I know about the
Japs. I was in Burma. You're not talking to—"

"O.K. O.K. I crawl for pardon. I forgot. You were
there. Kilroy Gilligan was there. O.K. Open a fresh box.
To go on. May I go on, General? We shelled the bastards
for days, burned them alive in the bunkers, and then they
counterattacked. Two days of counterattack. And we
mowed them down. I worked a spray gun myself. They
came hour after hour and we mowed them down, and I
don't mind telling you I was real scared. Yes, real scared.
They weren't trying to get anywhere that we think of as
anywhere. They were through and they just wanted to
die and to take us with them. So we killed them." His
voice was colder now. "Brave? Don't tell me about
bravery—"

"But I know all this," Gilligan said exasperatedly, as if
silence would lose him some kind of ground. "I was in
Burma. I saw it. Do you mean you ran away?"

"O.K. You were there. You were Kilroy." Muller's
eyes were staring ahead. "Jeeze, I can't help it if I was
there too. O.K. So we killed them all, about two thousand
of them, and when they were through and dead we
captured the colonel. He had been stunned by mortar
fire and when he came to and found he was a prisoner he
went out of his goddam mind and he knelt down and
gripped my legs and cried and asked me to kill him. He

begged me to shoot him, tried to drag my Colt out of its holster. And when I refused, and I'm telling you I wanted to put my hands around the guy's throat and give him a personal send-off, because yes, sure, I knew the bastard cared less than I did. How do I mean? Forget it, General. Anything but be a prisoner, he said, and would I shoot him, please, please. He and his troops had made our kind of bravery look like the boy scouts, and I hated the bastard for that, so I made him live. He ran around in a bunker all night, screaming and weeping, asking the sentries to shoot him, but I made the bastard live, while there was nothing I wanted more than to kill him myself, but I denied myself, because that was what he wanted more than anything, for me to kill him. And that's why I hated that guy." Muller was very worked up now, as if the smell of the rotting Japanese was again in his nostrils, and as if once more that special feeling of fear and hatred which Japanese military bravery had aroused in him was upon him. Not only had they had no pity for others, the Japanese, he said to Gilligan, but they made it look fine by having none at all for themselves. They had spoiled everything. "I made the bastard live and for three days he was out of his mind with it, screaming and sobbing, trying to hang himself with a piece of wire. That was my revenge, see. That's the worst thing I've ever done. The worst." He stopped speaking, knowing he had not been able to convey fully why it was the worst, for him.

"But you never ran away," Gilligan said, sardonic with his anger.

"No." Muller gripped Gilligan's arm again, urgent

with the inability to express what he could not express, his war with the Japanese which was going to go on inside him forever. "I never ran away. But that colonel threw me in some kind of way. I mean either soldiering is as total as they made it, or it's boy scouts like we did it. I should have let that colonel kill himself. That was his tradition and his right, but he lived instead. I saw to that, and he got used to it, got to like it—" anger cold and ferocious was in his voice again now—"and last time I saw the bastard, in the prisoner-of-war camp, he was taking a course in American business methods, getting ready for gracious living. Just another dollar-hunting bum. You couldn't get that guy to kill himself now not if you insured him for a million bucks. That's what I did to him. The Jap fight-to-the-death thing was the very tops. It was really way out, and I should have left it that way. But here it is. I've got it. There's no fun in killing a guy who's opening his shirt and laughing happily and saying 'put it right here,' is there?" He asked himself now in a shout, "*Is* there?"

He meant that the Japanese had defeated him by not caring about being killed, had more or less tyrannized over him forever by making death look nothing, whereas it was everything. Bravery for a Japanese would be to live, to disobey orders and live, to be called a coward and not care. They had bent everything until coming out of the battle alive was failure itself.

"So you think they were better than we were?" Gilligan asked bitterly. "Is that it? Is that your particular kind of trouble?" He wanted to laugh but could not manage it. He was too upset by feelings which Muller had aroused, and which he could not understand. It was as if

Muller had described the end of something. "You do think they were better than we were, don't you?"

"You ever fight to the death anywhere?" Muller asked, grinning tiredly. "Or do I see you around? No, we're here, alive. Don't talk to me about bravery. It's just a goddam English word to me since the war. It's over anyway. Some guy in Moscow will phone Washington and say, 'Let's have a fireball tonight.' I mean it's all over." He was surprising himself as he listened. "Yeah, the Japs ruined it all for me a long time ago, anyway, pre-bomb I mean. Mind you, I don't agree with what they did, dying like that. But I don't want to hear any more crap about bravery in battle from our end of the table. I hated the Japs for being so good at dying. That's why I punished that colonel. I was wrong."

"I don't know what the hell you're talking about anyway," said Gilligan with an angry sigh.

"You don't want to know, that's why," Muller said, not sure himself what he had been talking about, yet almost in sight of mysteries which had puzzled him always, problems of how dead a hero had to be.

"I've been thinking about that bull," Gilligan said in a cooler voice. "I've got to shoot it myself. There are plenty of other elephants—"

"I told you before I'm not discussing it further. This is my safari and I'm killing that bull, and we've got an agreement in writing, and I'm tired of you and your problem, pal. O.K.?"

"Listen to me, Muller—"

"Nuts. I've listened. Now quit the elephant saga or I'll finish up on a couch paying a guy money to tell me I love elephants. No more yap about being brave. I'm tired of it. Real tired. I'm a coward, a brave one, every day, like you—" he raised his cold voice again "—only I don't yammer about it all day. See? Cigarette?"

Nothing, though, seemed able to soothe Gilligan's unease. He felt that he no longer belonged to himself.

27

It was the young bull who first suspected that men were trailing them. He caught a sniff of man, just one faint sour sniff on a fresh, suddenly changing breeze, and his sense memory recognized it at once. He stopped dead in his ambling walk through heavy shade and sniffed on the breeze again, quivering, for he had known terror before, in a herd set upon by men with rifles, while still a growing calf. He moved about, his head raised, searching the breeze for that rotten special smell again, but it was gone. He moved slowly and massively under a tree and stood there, releasing an unexpected cascade of dung balls as a spasm of foreboding took hold of his enormous organism. The old bull was ripping down the canopy of a tree about a hundred yards away, unalarmed, secure. The young bull stood quite still under his tree and listened, sniffing the breeze which had changed again.

Halfway up a tree, frozen in an attitude of suspense,

Gavai kept his eyes on the young bull which was standing not a hundred yards away. He knew the elephant had heard or smelled him, knew it was worried, listening for one more sound, sniffing for one more scent. Gavai gripped the tree with his black legs crisscrossed with long white scratches, motionless, his bow held outward in his left hand. The young bull suddenly wheeled and went off at speed, in long swinging easy perambulation. Gavai heard him crashing through the trees, heard the other elephant, of which he had earlier caught a swift glimpse, joining in the great noise, and the noise went on, diminishing, dying in the distance. The sentry had done his work and given his warning. Gavai came down the tree in one leap. Chongu got up out of the thorns and signaled to Gilligan and Muller.

"The bastards have gone again," Gilligan complained.

"Who cares? We're on to them. We'll get them," Muller said. He was excited, but only showed it in the way his eyes flashed and glowed, in the way he kept gripping his rifle, as if promising it reward quite soon.

Having prepared himself by his confidences to Muller, having thus committed himself to facing what he most feared—the enormous trampling and screaming beast which had so confirmed his earlier terrors by that savage and brief destruction of his friend, Pratt—Gilligan was impatient for action. He had to have it over and done with as soon as possible. He was forcing the pace, nagging Jama, Muller, Chongu, and Gavai. It had to be today, the end of his battle; otherwise there would be another night to pass in darkness, lying on a bed trying to force sleep, and dreading sleep because of dreams. He was in such a condition of urgent tension now that Muller was trying to keep away from him, but watched him all the time. There was something almost sad about Gilligan's increasing anxiety to close with the elephant, and this was making Muller apprehensive and even afraid. He had begun to think of the old bull as a killer, as an experienced beast which knew what to do with its enemy which it was now seeking so hard to avoid. Already he had said, carefully, to Gilligan, Don't forget this is no ordinary elephant. It's cunning. It knows its stuff. You know that better than I do. Don't let's crowd it this way. You've got the trackers worried."

"Yes. Yes," Gilligan had agreed, again pathetic in this moment of doubt and worry. He was almost forgetting to be what he was, superior, experienced, learned in all the lore of the bush. He seemed to be starting to go to pieces, Muller thought. Muller began to wish he was alone to kill his elephant. Neither of them had yet seen the elephants, but were close on their tracks, on their too-soft dung, their platelike tracks in the shale. And the bush was getting thicker.

Gilligan was in pain, racked with muscular twinges which were like red hot needles piercing his flesh at times. He was depressed by what he was feeling, the first onslaught of age, and the worry of it, the humiliating nag of it had almost demoralized him. He was old and he was stupid, and he had said too much to this confident, aggressive companion he had, and he was full of shadowy and oppressive forebodings. He felt an envy of Muller which made him ashamed, and the knowledge that he was glad and grateful Muller was there with him was like some unavoidable acceptance of defeat.

'I'll do it,' he had decided as soon as that first letter

from Muller had come. 'I'll do it. This is my chance to settle the score.' He had for so long looked on all elephants as the enemy, as his humiliators, that it did not seem out of the ordinary for him to go to that picture of the old bull on the wall of his shack and say, "Your bloody number's up. Or mine is. But one of us has to go, and I intend it to be you."

Perhaps it had been wrong to confide as he had done in Muller, the result of despondency and low health, but however he looked at it now, he had had to do it. He had signed on for the duration with those words. He kept on reliving the scene, with Muller lying on his bed listening, while he, Gilligan, pulled out that vile secret and showed it. In a way Muller was a good chap for the way he had responded. 'But I've finished something of myself,' Gilligan fretted. 'Trust is trust, yet once you give way to it you're done, you've lost yourself,' and he had never done it before. Now, though, he was going to stand in front of that bull, whose great bloody tusks he remembered glistening redly for a moment before his flight, and he was going to smash it down, forever, and then he had done everything, arrived. 'I'll have arrived,' he thought. 'I'll be a different man.' He had no doubt that he would be a very different man. There was nothing like actually *doing* a thing. You could not lie about it. You had to *do* it. Only then could you believe yourself, and five hundred dead lions, a thousand rhinoceroses, a plain full of dead buffalo could not bring that about for him, never had been able to. 'So here we are, chum,' he thought.

He had still not conveyed anything like the size of his mania to Muller, of the millions of thoughts he had had about this one scene as compared with the other, this one where he slew, and that other where the elephant had slain. It was so important, so big, that no words could convey what he had suffered for years.

Now he was starting to worry that darkness would come just as the trackers found the elephants. Chongu had tried to tell him that the elephants were not running away and were not aware that they were being trailed.

"I know when an elephant is frightened," Gilligan stormed at him. "Don't try and teach me my work, Chongu. You've scared them and they're running."

"Quit riding the guys, Gill," Muller complained. "You've been on their necks all day. Relax." Gilligan just stared at him with his hard, worried blue eyes.

Muller himself was in that intoxicating state just before danger when a man knows he can meet it and triumph over it, and have pleasure as well. He had lived the moment so many times in rehearsal in his skull, the sighting, the marking of the spot, the swing up of his heavy rifle, dead on it would be, that ivory bead of sight, and then with a curling of his finger he would send the hurtling iron message right to the center of the small target in the ponderous skull. He was more patient than Gilligan, poor Gilligan who was knocking himself out to lay a ghost he had manufactured for himself. Along with his excitement, though, Muller was feeling a certain amount of fear, which was like salt, adding savor to the thing. For many miles they went in uneasy silence, and when darkness began to fall Gilligan seemed spent, pale, and grieved. They made camp among some tall boulders. Chongu said the elephants were about two miles ahead, at least.

"How far do you reckon we might have to go after these goddam elephants, Gill?" Muller asked.

"Don't know," Gilligan said. "They've got a lot of country to move in. Once you come into this country up here you can feel swallowed up. That's what's great about it, I suppose, and what keeps it free. I wouldn't mind dying in this piece of country."

"Yeah? Well let's talk about living instead. You're in need of a drink, that's what."

The whisky did taste good. Gilligan drank it neat, throwing it down like water.

"We'll get them tomorrow," he said. "You'll see."

28

IT WAS NOT TILL AFTER NOON the next day that they saw the elephants, unexpectedly, and they went to ground at once, Muller following Gilligan. They lay still in the dry, grayish rank grass, their eyes on the beasts about a quarter of a mile away in a clearing. Muller took his binoculars out of the pocket of his bush shirt and studied the big bull, saying, "Jeeze, he's bigger than a tank. And get a load of those tusks. The other one's big too, but nothing like number one. Boy, I can't wait."

"Then wait." Gilligan reached out his hand for the binoculars, put them to his eyes, and was pleased to find that Muller's eyes were weaker than his own. He had to refocus the glasses and said to Muller, "You need a pair of hornrimmed spectacles, do you know that, Muller. You've got bad eyesight."

"You old bastard," Muller said, annoyed but confiding. "It's true too. My eyes are pretty shot but I can't wear a

pair of goddam glasses. Vanity. You're a cunning old
bastard, you never miss a trick, do you?" Gilligan looked
at him and smiled.

"I knew you had bad sight days ago," he said. "You
can tell the way a fellow looks at a thing when it's far
off. *You* look at a thing like that, forcing yourself to
see it. You nearly have to close your eyes."

"But I can shoot all right, eh? Can you shoot better?"

"You're not bad, considering." He called to Chongu
who was lying down ahead with Gavai. "Keep still, will
you? Where's Jama?"

"Here," said Jama from some reeds on the right.

"Bwana, you bastard," Gilligan shouted. "You mind
your manners, Jama, or by God I'll give you a boot up
the arse, do you hear me?" and, his temper expended, he
spoke in Ki-Swahili, ordering Jama to call him Bwana.
Muller put his face down into the grass, murmuring,
"The guy'll strangle you one of these days, Gill, with
that Bwana thing."

"What did you say?" Gilligan asked him sharply.

"I said, 'Oh, God, please make Jama call Gilligan Bwana
Gilligan.' Like a prayer kind of thing."

"Very amusing indeed." Gilligan felt for wind with a
wet finger and then with broken dried grass which he
threw into the air. "That's our way," he said. "We'll go
around that way and come out on them near those trees.
Ready?"

"I'll say I'm ready," said Muller, rising. They all moved
quietly over to the left, heading into the thorn trees.

It was about a mile walk to where Gilligan considered
they could move in on the elephants in security. He and

Chongu and Gavai watched the breeze nervously, for it was erratic, a hot eddying breeze which sometimes faded out into hot, glaring stillness again. Gilligan was feeling a vengeful and coldly willful confidence, and a doubt as well.

"I want to take on the big bull," he whispered to Muller, and he looked shocked when Muller shook his head and said, "No. It's mine. I've got to have that bastard for myself. Sorry, pal. I want that bull."

"No. I want him. I have more reason. I've got to have him. You know why. Come on, you have the other one. The big one's mine."

Muller stopped. "This is no time for a goddam conference about your fixations or your rights, Gill," he said. "The big one's mine, and I want him." He showed his teeth, suddenly all urgency and will. "That's all," he said. "*I'm* paying. I've come a long way and it's my bull. I don't want to beat the gums any more about you and elephants. See? Don't start making me mad. I want to be cool and ready. That's it." He moved off then, leaving Gilligan standing there incensed, and glad. Chongu and Gavai were well ahead and they knelt down now, signaling to Gilligan with their lips and chins. He ran forward silently on the sand in his soft rubber-soled suede boots. It was no time for Somali sandals now.

"Look," Chongu said in a faint whisper. He lifted his chin and pointed with it to a herd of elephants about two hundred yards beyond the two bulls. There must have been over fifty of them, red and gray and shining with mud and sunlight. Muller came up and knelt on one knee beside Gilligan, murmuring, "Jeeze, what a view.

It's worth everything to see that." Muller's joy in this sight made Gilligan feel proud, as if he owned Africa and it had come up to expectation for this stranger.

Muller was enchanted, in that peculiar way of the hunter when he gazes at the marvelous thing he is going to kill, in a kind of terrible love for the wild beast whose time he has measured, a last look at the peace he has pursued and which he has come to end. His eyes were glistening and his hands were beginning to tremble so that his mind was enjoying the wonderful sight before him and wondering if he would tremble in that important moment when he squinted down the rifle barrel at his victim.

Gilligan was sulking over his last words with Muller. He now wanted to kill the big bull. He knew he must do it. He could not come away from here without doing it. And then he knew that that must have been really why he had accepted Muller as a client who would pay for the safari up here. Any elephant was an elephant for Muller. But this bull whose bloody tusks shone so often in his restless sleep was the last part of him which he had never controlled. He had wanted to come back here for years, to this place where his enemy lived, fear.

As if he had tasted Gilligan's thoughts, as if they had come out of Gilligan's head like rays and entered his own, Muller turned to him and said in a low voice, "You want an elephant. Kill one. Kill as many as you like. It's just an *elephant* you need, Gill. O.K.? But leave the big bull to me. Don't be a lousy bastard now when we're at the end of the safari. You promised me that big bastard, didn't you, and I've come a long way and I want to shoot it and skin it. Can't you—"

"*Skin it*," Gilligan said impatiently. "You're off your head. Are you still talking about skinning it? We're miles from the trucks. It's too big a job." He had just laughed when Muller had first told him of his plan to skin the elephant, to preserve the skin, to take it back to America, and to present it to the museum to which he had promised it in his home town.

"All right," Muller whispered ferociously. "All right. Forget the goddam skinning for now. But I want to go ahead and knock the bastard down, the big one."

Chongu, Gavai, and Jama were in a little silent crouching group watching the two white men having their whispered argument.

Gilligan crawled close to Muller and looked into his eyes. Staring right into those blue eyes Muller saw pain, and, with the flared nostrils and the curious downward twist of Gilligan's mouth, an expression of intense suffering and quiet insanity. He forgot the elephants, the plains, and the trees all about them, forgot even where they were for a moment or two as he wondered why men bothered themselves so much about things which did not matter, but which were going to matter forever to the whole human race, this insanity about making things matter, acts of imagination become facts for filing in the courage box.

"Listen, Gill," he said. "All this crap about me filming you shooting the bull. All this torture. To hell with it. I tell you you've been sick for years. There are millions of things *I* can't do, because I'm scared to do them, and I'm never going to do them—" he leaned forward, his mouth nearer to Gilligan's ear, and in a sort of whispered shout, went on "—and I don't give a goddam who knows it. I don't care. Why don't you be really brave and leave the elephant alone and stay scared and live with it. That's the real guts, you know. Not doing it. That's growing up."

"You're a cunning bastard, aren't you, Muller?" Gilligan was chuckling silently at him, his shoulders shaking. "That was good, that bit. And then I say, 'That's it. That's what I want to hear. Fine. So you go and kill the old bull, because I never thought of any of that stuff you said until now.' But you silly bastard, Muller, don't you understand that I've done all that, tried all that, tried to pull out of this pride thing and face it as something that doesn't matter. But it's not true. I know that until I kill this bull here I'm never going to be any good. I'll stay a liar."

"Ah, goddam you," Muller exclaimed, shaking his rifle in exasperation. "Goddam you. You're trying to cheat me. Isn't that worse than all this crap you have about you and elephants? You start all this stuff now when we're on top of the herd—" While Muller went on, Gilligan saw what he had been doing up to now, from when he had told Muller he must shoot that bull for himself. He had been arranging things in such a way that Muller would argue him out of shooting the elephant, so that he would be able gracefully to stand back and not have to deal with his demon after all.

"Bwana, the elephants are moving," Chongu called.

"You see, you crazy bastard." Muller's voice had angry grief in it, like that of a boy finally denied something he has wheedled to get. He jumped to his feet and began to race across the sand. Immediately the Africans got up and went after him. The herd, in a rolling, shambling, rocking gathering of shining red and gray colossi were moving toward the thin forest in the distance. The old bull and his friend were following them. Gilligan got up and ran after Muller. Shame and fury were upon him, and he was not sure any more of why he was really here in this wilderness. It was the American who had wanted to come to this wilderness, and had come many thousands of miles, journeying all that way to fire a piece of metal into one particular beast, and now he was running after it.

Chongu stood and waited for Gilligan. "Bwana," he said, "they have not smelled us. They are not afraid. They are simply moving away to another place. But if the other Bwana runs too close to them they will discover us."

"Yes. I know that. The Bwana is a *m'geni* and does not know these things," Gilligan said. "He cannot wait." He turned and saw Muller kneeling with his .500 poised half-way up to his shoulder, his eyes on the big bull which had stopped moving, staring as if hypnotizing it, ready to fling the rifle butt into his shoulder and take his aim. The two bulls were about five hundred yards away. Gilligan ran quickly to Muller and said, "What are you going to do, try a few ranging shots or open barrage fire on them? They're a quarter of a mile away, you silly bastard."

Muller, his gray eyes shining with actual hatred, looked up at Gilligan who was bending over him.

"If you sound off just one more time to me, Gilligan, about what to do or how to do it, after the last few days we've had together, by Christ I'll kill you. Now shut that goddam trap of yours, and I'm asking you as a favor. See?" He was in such a condition of nervous excitement that he was almost panting. Gilligan was smiling, shaking with small, silent laughter.

"All right," he said. "All right. Keep cool or that rifle of yours will go off in your hand. Go and shoot the bull, the old one. He's yours. I'll back you up from behind. You don't want any advice from me, eh? You know everything. You know exactly what to do. You want to hear nothing from me. Right?"

"Correct. I know just what to do, where to put the shot, exactly where, in fact. Don't you worry." He held out his right hand. "I know how you want that bull, Gill. Thanks. Don't give me any crap about being embarrassed. Just shake my goddam hand and don't suffer about it. You're so full of limey neuroses it hurts me." Gilligan had to take his hand and shake it, smiling in self-defense as he did it. Muller got up.

"The wind is right, Bwana," Chongu said.

"Fine. I'm behind you, Muller," Gilligan said. "It's all yours." They glanced into each other's eyes.

"Now I'll show you some shooting, Gill," Muller told him.

"Show it to the bull, not me."

"O.K." Muller went forward, safety catch off, the heavy double-barreled rifle at the high port, the barrels slightly out to the left, his right elbow stuck out so that he could whip the red-rubber-padded butt up into his shoulder in a single movement. Gilligan moved out to the right, about five yards behind, a sudden rush of sweat coming out on his body as he realized what he was doing, as he went forward to face the big bank account of private fear. His mouth was quite dry.

The herd were well back from the two unsuspecting

bulls, about a quarter of a mile beyond, Gilligan guessed. The old bull was in some scattered trees, clearly visible, his great head raised, his trunk waving among branches. The young bull was about a hundred yards beyond him to the left, standing as if pondering over some problem, the sunlight dull on the drying red mud smeared across his back and sides.

How well Muller moved, Gilligan thought, watching the tall, agile American striding softly forward, his sensitivity at work through the rubber soles of his bush boots, his wary eyes on the bulls, and flickering on the sand before him as well as he watched for dry and dead branches to avoid.

Three hundred yards. Two hundred yards. Muller went more slowly now, beginning to crouch slightly. Behind Gilligan, Jama strolled along chewing a piece of grass, the .318 on his shoulder. Gavai was darting about like a black flea in the bushes away on the right behind Gilligan. Just behind Gilligan's shoulder, his long spear held ready in his hand, his large black eyes wide and unwinking and fixed on the old bull, was Chongu. The approach, led by Muller, was screened by low bush and dead twisted trees which the white ants had chewed into shells of grayish paperlike substance. At about seventy yards, and just as Gilligan was going to whisper for a halt, Muller stopped. Everyone stopped with him.

In a dream of his own, all of them forgotten, his eyes wide and full of trance, Gilligan looked at the huge towering bull he had not seen for so many years. Why had he not come himself, years ago, to have done with all this stupid and complicated idiocy he had allowed to take him over? Muller had slowly turned his head to catch

Gilligan's eyes. They looked at each other. Muller winked and Gilligan nodded, and as Muller turned his head he was lifting the rifle into his shoulder, and just then the big bull slowly turned and ambled off.

Gilligan heard his own breath being expelled in a long, quiet sigh, and again he began to build up the necessary tension and readiness. Muller looked at him, and the bull stopped and began to tear some greenery from a high slender tree. The range was now about a hundred yards. The wind was still all right. Muller jerked his head forward. Gilligan nodded. Muller moved forward, one step at a time, feeling the sand with each knowing foot as he went, Gilligan following. The bull turned to face them, looking suddenly cunning, though innocent; looking as if he knew Gilligan had come back here after so long. And Gilligan, although he knew that the bull could not see them or smell them, shivered for a second or two, as if the bull's little eyes were staring at him alone and saying, "So you've come at last, have you?"

'Put your bloody rifle up, man, and get it over,' Gilligan shouted silently, staring at Muller. Then he looked at the big bull, at the long heavy yellow tusks which had budded generations ago, before the first tiny white man had appeared up here from the coast with his beads, his *posho*, his two thousand years of square and circle in his little skull, the germ carrier of ordered restlessness with an appetite which not all the planets would ever satisfy.

Why not just raise his rifle, sight, and shoot it himself? There it was, waiting for him, Gilligan, looking at him, Gilligan, and saying, "Well, here I am, no blood on these tusks now, but it's there, isn't it? Shoot me. Shoot the rest of yourself. I'm here, ready."

'Get your rifle up, man, will you?' Gilligan was in agony, watching Muller, who was crouched and with his eyes fixed on the elephant. Other statues stood frozen in the glowing heat, Gavai there, Chongu here, Jama casual, manipulating the piece of grass with his teeth. Then, slowly, Muller brought his rifle up into his shoulder, got himself set, while Gilligan, his habitual hunter's spirit counting the seconds, worked out without knowing it everything that Muller was doing. The eye down the barrel, the adjustment of the barrel until the black raised V of the backsight began to center the white bead of the foresight, and then the eye, contented now, reaching out beyond the ready sights to the tiny area of elephant through which the hole must be punched by the pill which carried tons of stunning power.

Hours seemed to have passed in this hot glaring silence while the statues watched the foremost statue of Muller who was pointing that rifle at the age-old monster who seemed to be waiting for his death. And then Muller lowered the rifle slowly and hung his head slightly, and from where he stood Gilligan could see him swallowing, and the rifle trembling. He took several long, slow steps until he was nearer Muller, who looked at him over his shoulder and smiled wearily. He could not keep his rifle steady enough to satisfy himself. He was having a crisis about his tension. It was his wry smile which Gilligan's instinct told him explained what was the matter. When he had his sights on the small area of the beast's skull he could not keep the rifle still enough to give him that necessary comfort which preceded the deadly shot. So he started to have another try at it. Jama was rolling his eyes in mock despair to amuse Chongu, and Gilligan saw it and shook his fist at him in silent rage, and Jama was solemn again.

Now Muller got the foresight on to the right fold in that terrific head, drew his slow breath as he pulled the butt into his shoulder, all the muscles of his arms doing what they should, right hand tightening as the forefinger poised itself to obey on the trigger, left hand pulling in with the right until the rifle was set, and still he could not stop the tremor which made the foresight waver, and there was nothing he could do about it, and curses for himself mounted up in silence, for Gilligan must be laughing behind him. He had courage enough not to say to himself, 'To hell with it. I can't go on like this. I'll chance it,' and fire wildly. He brought the rifle down again, and by now was in such a temper, such a state of angry shame that his nervous excitement was heightened, and he looked at Gilligan with raging, hopeless eyes, pantomiming his anger, and Gilligan pantomimed back, raising his eyes until they were back in his head, and then he brought them down and glared at Muller. And the bull turned and began to join the young one, and Muller watched them in a mood of despair, and Gilligan watched Muller with a piercing blue stare of contempt, He went up to Muller and said in a hissing whisper, "Will you for God's sake show us that piece of shooting? What's the matter with you?"

Muller was too cast down to be angry. He shrugged his shoulders and let out a long exhalation of breath, sweat shining on his face.

"Sorry, Gill," he whispered. "Everything's set and I just can't keep my goddam rifle still I'm so scared of missing, and then maybe it's the look of that big bastard.

He looks so old and sad. I thought he was watching me."

"Look, Muller, this is ridiculous. Get on to him again, fire when you're ready, and I'm here behind you. Let him have it before he starts giving you advice himself about what to do. You stood there so long that he'd recognize you anywhere in the future."

"O.K. Let's start this goddam thing all over again," Muller replied despondently. He was in misery with himself. He had been so near ecstasy in those moments before sighting that he seemed to have lost control over his nerves altogether. He wanted to explain everything to the angry Gilligan, to talk it all away, but he was dumb with his frustration. So once more they began to stalk the elephants.

The sun was well down when once more they began the noiseless, creeping approach until Muller was again about fifty or so yards from the elephant, and once more the elephant was facing him.

'Now shoot him, superman, or I'll bloody well shoot you,' Gilligan said soundlessly to Muller. He was worn out.

Like a sudden, sharp clap of thunder against the heavy silence, Muller's rifle went off, and, under the smashing blow of that powerful bullet, the many tons of towering, mud-smeared elephant shook and went backward just as the long, pillarlike legs began to buckle. And the young bull seemed to have gone mad.

29

"HE'S DOWN. HE'S DOWN," Muller was chanting, his rifle held out in front of him, his clenched right fist pushing downward to the earth, as if forcing the shaken, wounded bull to hurry his collapse. Muller's eyes were opened wide, his lips drawn back from his white teeth in an expression of feral joy and his face was shining with sweat. Gilligan saw the slow and tremendous collapse of the bull even while his whole mind was spending this second in studying, terrified, the herd of elephants milling toward Muller and himself. They were about two hundred yards away now, veering, screaming, while the young bull, as if sure he had found the cause of that sudden explosion which had struck down his charge and friend, had ceased his desperate and aimless charges among the trees and was heading toward Gilligan's right.

In the next second, while he was screaming, "Look

out. Look out, Muller. Look out," Gilligan saw the big
stricken bull collapse onto his knees and stay there, his
colossal head falling forward as if dragged down by the
sheer weight of his yellow tusks.

"You missed. You missed," Gilligan shouted, crouching now, adding, "Look out. Get down. Down. Down,
you stupid bastard," for Muller, mad with the killing
fever, was about to fire another round into the bull's
head, as if he had no idea of the trembling in the earth,
as if he had not taken in the sight that had almost
paralyzed Gilligan's senses, for the whole herd was
charging at them. All else to right and left, all but the
sight of the trumpeting elephants coming straight at
them, was obliterated from Gilligan's sight. He was on
his knees, his right thumb so obedient over the years
having already slipped the safety catch back and forth
twice as hope dissolved into fear and then came back
again. "Down, you silly bastard," he screamed at Muller,
and Muller went down on one knee and then, as if he
had understood at last, cried, "Jeezus, look." He fell flat
on his face and Gilligan went down too.

Whatever sense it was that so many years of experience had sharpened in Gilligan's body, for all of a
hunter's peculiar eyes are in his body, he was right about
the fallen bull. That great head, a monument of cellular
bone, like a tough, springy sponge inside which the small
brain sent its sparse and uncomplicated messages to a
couple of appetites, had absorbed the titanic blow of the
iron slug. The brain was intact, and before he went down
on his face Gilligan had seen the gleam of blood above
the small area behind which lay the tunnel through the
skull leading to the brain. Muller had missed. The tons

of instantaneously delivered shock behind the .500 bullet
had knocked the bull unconscious.

There must have been a couple of hundred charging
tons of elephant coming past the fallen bull now, and
the earth was quivering all about the puny men hiding
in terror in the gray, starved grass. Gilligan pressed his
hands over his ears, every atom of him awake and urgent
and awaiting the crushing fall of the platelike feet, hundreds of them almost upon them now. He heard Muller's
choked voice shouting, "No. No. No," in anguish as the
herd came toward them in their useless hiding place.
There was nothing to do but cower and wait to be
burst open, or picked up and hurled, or knelt upon.
Gilligan heard his own thin whining as he let out his
breath while the thunder of the racing elephants went
over him, leaving him alive and unhurt. Sweat had burst
out all over his flesh as if forced through his pores under
pressure. It turned cold at once as he heard the herd
turning some distance behind him. With one sly, terrified
eye he saw Muller rising through the red dust swirling
before him, and he shouted, as if giving a command
through shellfire, "Get *down*, you bastard," and Muller
went down with his hands over his face, for the herd
was coming back in another rumble and screaming. They
had gone mad. The herd went over them again and this
time Gilligan heard himself moaning prayers and supplica-
tions. The ground heaved under his face as one elephant's
weight went past him by a couple of inches. He felt he
was fainting, yet he believed he would survive. Neither
of the two men moved now. They lay quite still as
the frantic herd rushed on toward the fallen bull. "Don't
move, Muller," Gilligan screamed into his own hands,

into the sand. The ground was still throbbing and heaving as the elephants milled and surged about the fallen bull.

Gilligan sucked in his quavering breath, demoralized now that the terrible experience was over, but awaiting another charge of the screeching beasts ahead. He did not want to look at them again. He only wanted to hear them go away now. He was limp and shivering, stretched full length on the sand and listening to the venomous calls and cries of the herd which seemed to be running about in a circle of panic. It was as if he were falling asleep now, his mind stunned, for he could not think. All he could do was let pointless and crazy thoughts stream through his head as fast as they came. His mind was trying to get ready to work again, to take part once more in a meshing with the shaking flesh which had had its way for a few minutes of panic and terror. He looked up, swallowing hard in his dry throat, and the fallen bull was gone. It was not there. There was churned sand. He could see the movements of many elephants in the far trees, and then they vanished. The plain and the low hills were empty.

"It's gone," he exclaimed. "The bull's gone with them."

Muller got up then, slowly, as white-faced as Gilligan, each of them looking at the other and thinking, 'By God, you don't look so good, mister,' and 'That shook you all right, chum, eh?'

A horrible, weary smile came onto Muller's face, almost evil, for he was too shattered to complete the ghastly effort of it. He looked like a man who had surrendered to total fear, and he was smiling because Gilligan looked so dreadful and old and spent just then.

"What's gone?" Muller said stupidly, still trying to grin. "You look shot. Real shot."

"Shot?" Gilligan snarled. "What about the bull? Is that shot? Look, you bloody big mouth." He pointed to where the bull had been. After the blow it had been struck by that bullet in the head a couple of minutes ago, the bull had no right to be gone. It was Jama who explained it.

30

"THEY TAKE HIM. They lift him. Take him," Jama was yelling as he loped up to them through the sand and scrub, the .318 in his hand. He was laughing with fear and excitement as he reached the spot where the two drained white men were kneeling.

"Swahili," Gilligan commanded, looking at him sternly. "I want to know what you saw. Say it in Swahili."

"Say it anyway you goddam well like," Muller shouted hysterically. "What happened?" He was shaking his fists in Jama's face.

"Where's Chongu?" Gilligan demanded.

"To hell with Chongu." Muller waved his clenched fist at Jama. "What happened? Where's my bull?"

In English and Ki-swahili Jama told them what he had seen after the elephants had charged back over them. He said several of the elephants had lifted the wounded bull to his feet and had then held him up and walked him off while the herd, led by the screeching young bull, had made their two charges.

"You're a liar," Gilligan snapped at him, even though he had once heard of such a thing happening from an old elephant hunter gone under the earth these many years. "How many elephants lifted him? Now don't lie to me or by God I'll hurt you." He was trembling, with rage he thought, though he was wrong. Only now had the shock of their experience reached his center and taken proper shape. He was thinking, 'How did we live through that? How?'

He believed Jama now, nodding as he listened. Then he and Muller got to their feet and went forward to look at the place where the bull had lain in the sand. Gilligan could just walk it. He felt old and soaked with pain and time and a curious sort of despair, a tremendous despondency. He lost all interest in the affair, even while his eyes saw the deep tunnels made by tusks in the sand where the elephants had dug them beneath the huge wounded bull. Jama described everything and the sand told the rest of the story. They had raised him up, this survivor of generations, this curio of pre-white Africa, had shouldered themselves against him, perhaps tenderly, perhaps sorrowfully, and had held him up and walked him painfully away while the rest of the elephants had swarmed and screamed and stampeded all around him.

After that Gilligan had to sit down on a rotten tree and wonder why he had no more interest in any of this. Perhaps a cigarette would help, and a drink. It took him a long time of fumbling to get the flask of whisky out of the patch pocket of his bush shirt, Muller watching him closely.

"You sure look shot right now," Muller was drawling, and like a terrier Gilligan was up and at his throat, gripping his throat and yelling, "You say that to me once more, Muller, and I'll bloody well shoot you." Muller did not move, did not raise a hand. He let Gilligan grip his throat while he stared into his eyes and smiled another of those ugly, tired smiles, and Gilligan, ashamed, his eyes glittering, took his hands away and went and sat down again. Jama, his eyes like two big black heads, watched everything, and then suavely went on telling about what he had seen.

"Go away," Gilligan said. "Go and look for Chongu and that little black bastard with the bow and arrow. Go on."

"Yes. Shove off for a while, Jama," Muller said. Jama sauntered away, sulking, muttering.

"You put your goddam hands on me like that again, Gilligan, and I'll—"

"Ah, shut up, will you?" Gilligan looked about two hundred years old. He looked wearily at Muller and drank some whisky. It was so good to taste, so fine to feel it hitting his stomach like fire, that he had to bow his head in pleasure and gratitude, holding the flask out to Muller. "Here," he said. "Drink some. We're both very lucky to be alive." And Muller came over and took the flask and had a drink of the whisky. His hand was shaking so much that he watched it for a second or two, smiling at it.

"Yeah," he said. "That's right. I forgot that. You ever heard of elephants doing that before? I mean carrying off a wounded one. He was dying. He was dead, not dying. You mean to tell me that elephants carry off a dead bull like that?"

"They want to give him a decent funeral, that's why," Gilligan murmured disgustedly, leaning his elbows on his knees and scowling at the trees ahead. "They've got shovels back there in the forest and that's why they carry a dead bull away like that. Be your bloody age, will you?" He looked contemptuously at Muller. "You and your shooting," he went on. "You missed and he was stunned, and they took him off. That's what."

"I couldn't have missed," Muller said, not believing himself, knowing he had missed. "You saw him go down."

"It'll be dark in an hour," Gilligan said, sighing. "That's that, chum. It was a nice safari."

"*Was?* How about getting off your ass and making like you were the great white hunter, pal? I want that bull." He turned and shouted to Jama, who was moving about some two hundred yards from them. "You ready, Jama? We're going on."

'I'm done,' Gilligan was thinking, pains running through his racked body. 'I'm done and this bastard is going to kill me if I don't look out. I'm done.'

All the strength and confidence had come back into Muller now. He hated that bull for living, and every moment it was moving farther out of his life, he who had knocked it down in that magic second of power. Jama came running, saying that Chongu was dead. Gilligan put his head in his hands and moaned.

"Christ," said Muller, moved. "Chongu? Dead?"

"We'd better go and see." Gilligan made himself get to his feet, still in the daze, that half light of interest in what was going on. He felt as if he never wanted to see another rifle, another safari. He was done.

Chongu was a reddish-brown stain on the earth, gritty,

bloody cloth tangled in the stain, his wild mop of hair like a reddish plant in the sand. Half the herd must have gone over him.

"*You* should have been there, not Chongu," Gilligan said huskily to Jama, hate and grief in his eyes. Then some tears formed in his eyes and he walked away.

"What Bwana say?" Jama asked Muller, suspicious and grim.

"And where's that little guy?" Muller asked Jama. "That hunter? You see him?"

"What Bwana say to me?" Jama asked again, for he knew by the look in Gilligan's eyes that something insulting had been said to him.

"Did you hear what I *said* to you?" Muller shouted at him, a Bwana at last with Jama. "Where's that hunter guy!"

"He gone. Run away," said Jama dully, his interest gone now that he could not get an answer to that important question. "Bwana hate me. He hate Jama."

Turning on his heel, Muller shouted to Gilligan, "We'd better get moving if we want that bull. I'm not leaving him. I'm going to get him. And don't forget all that crap you used to spout to me about a wounded beast, eh? Play the game, old chap, and all that sort of thing, you know, what, eh?"

"Tomorrow. Tomorrow," Gilligan called back. "Give yourself a chance, will you?" He never wanted to see an elephant again. There was some kind of curse on them where he, Gilligan, was concerned. But he knew he would have to go.

"Now, not tomorrow," Muller shouted, walking up to him, Jama following. "You get another shot of that whisky in you and let's move. I'm going to have that bull even if I have to walk for a whole year." He had taken over, and he knew it, he knew it by the way Gilligan said, "I'd just like a cigarette first. You want one?"

"Thanks."

"A bloody impudent swine like that one over there can live and a marvelous fellow like Chongu gets killed," Gilligan mourned bitterly, glowering at Jama, who was sitting under a tree. "You mean to tell me that's justice? Eh?" He looked into Muller's eyes.

Muller was studying him, watching his eyes. "Are you trying to load Chongu onto me?" he asked belligerently. "What are you looking at me like that for? You feel all right?"

"Nothing's been any good since you came," Gilligan said.

"You smoke your cigarette and then we'll go after that bull. And then we'll have a few drinks," Muller told him, "and then you can cool off. Now quit this snide and this bitching, will you, pal? All right. Chongu's dead. Too bad."

Gilligan looked at him, his eyebrows raised, almost peering at him. "You don't care about Chongu, do you?" he said. "It doesn't mean a bloody thing to you, does it? Admit it, so I'll know what I thought from the start. You're just a bloody machine, chum, that's all. A mouth on two legs. A big head. Too bad, you say? He was better than you, Chongu." Tears came again into his eyes. Muller looked uncomfortable, angry and shifty.

"I'm going ahead," he said. "You come on when you feel sensible." It worked. As Muller walked off, Gilligan followed, slinging his rifle, his head bent. Jama followed.

31

THEY SLEPT OUT THAT NIGHT. Just as the sun went down Gilligan took the .318 from Jama and casually shot a gerenuk which was standing in a hollow.

"Gut it and bring it in," he told Jama. He seemed to have no interest in what he was saying. There was a terrible pain in his side and behind his knees. He felt as if he had a malaria coming on. Muller was a couple of hundred yards ahead, standing where he had stopped to watch Gilligan shoot the buck.

"Are we going to have another one of those epic marches?" Gilligan called to him. "You can't read signs now, chum, not even with your bloody eyesight."

"Never mind my eyesight," Muller cried back at him.

"Well, if you want to eat you'd better kip down with us here, because this is camp," Gilligan replied. To Jama he said "*Tanganeze moto. Piga chakula, na chai.*" And while Jama obediently went off to bring firewood, Gilligan lay down under a dead tree and more or less became unconscious, snoring as he lay there. Muller, who had come back, stood over him and smiled at him with a kindly sneer.

"That's right," he said. "Be your age. You're old. Fine. No harm in that. But you've had it."

He sat down and lit a cigarette. A thin cool breeze chilled the sweat on him and his brow felt like cold stone in a few seconds. He watched Jama laying the fire.

"Your Bwana's tired, Jama," he said. "You hear him snoring?"

"He's not my Bwana," Jama hissed fiercely, turning from his crouched position over the sputtering flames. "He hate me. He hate Somali mans. He have not cattles, no sheeps, nottings. *Laikin* he tink he is like king." He imitated Gilligan's sharp voice of command. "Go do dat. Do dis. Go dere. Come here. He bloody fool. Not my Bwana."

Muller smiled sardonically and said nothing, and Jama, who had been feeling his plan about in his mind for days, felt he must speak at last.

"You hate me, Bwana?" he asked Muller, his keen eyes suddenly piercing as they watched Muller's smile. "You tink I no good mans?"

"You're a jerk," said Muller, "but I don't hate you. Why should I hate you? Hate. Hate. Don't you know any other word?" He was sick of Jama. He wished Aganaza were here. Now there was a real useful guy with a heart, not like this one who had said, "Jama first. Jama come in first," after that crucifying march.

"Jerk?" Jama said suspiciously (he pronounced it "jerrick"). "What is jerk?"

"A jerk is a brilliant guy, Jama. A real, solid, likable guy, that's what a jerk is. Why, you don't like being a jerk?"

"Is English word?"

"American."

"Ah." Now was the time. America. "You take Jama America?" he said, looking into Muller's ironical gaze. "I want go America, school, get rich. Nottings here for Jama. You take me America?" The great yearning which had appeared in his eyes almost got through Muller's curtain of irony. He felt sorry for the poor guy. Even here, in this roasting wilderness belonging to the elephants, you found a guy waiting for his visa to the States. He was never going to forgive Jama for turning down the freedom he had given him, when he picked him up in the desert that day, and for going back into the employ of the maniac who had thrown him there.

"No," he said. "I won't."

"You no take me America?" Jama frowned at him.

"No."

A radiant smile spread over Jama's face. It was all solved, this worry which had been with him for so many days. He was not going to America. He had longed for it, but he could not go. A dark weight was lifted from his mind. "I make tea," he said.

"You're not only a jerk," Muller said, puzzled and irritated, "you're nuts as well." Jama had unslung the battered kettle and the haversack containing tin cups and tea.

"Nuts?" he said.

"Nuts," said Muller. "That's better than being a jerk. That's really human, being nuts. Like me. I'm nuts. Your Bwana's even more nuts. See?"

Jama nodded as if he understood. "I get water," he said.

"Where's the water?"

"Bwana Gilligan see it before dark. Is why he stop here and shoot buck."

"Yeah?" Gilligan knew his stuff, you had to hand him that, knowing where water was in this goddam chunk of hell they had traveled into. "Did he know there was a buck here waiting as well?" Jama admired Gilligan. That was why Jama hated Gilligan.

"No. He not know that," Jama said solemnly. "Is luck."

"O.K. Fine. Now you make tea and sling some hash and let me smoke my cigarette, hey? How about that?"

He lay on his back and looked at the stars and felt the grateful sigh of his body, for he was far more tired and dispirited just now than ever before. He knew it was not merely the electrical effect of the two forces meeting in continual and infuriating heat, himself and Gilligan, which made him feel this spentness just now. It was the soakage of isolation, the looking inward into self which wilderness brings on, and which had been ensnaring him into a closer self-inspection than usual. He had often thought of himself as a head case, as one in touchy, angry conflict with everything he had been brought up to consider "the world." Rich, he had always been able to have ten of everything, and ended by wanting none. He hated his houses, his pictures, his books, his collections of this and that, and left them standing, going off to Rio for the carnival, Venice for a few drinks, Kashmir to shoot an ibex, Hong Kong because it was Hong Kong. He had never let anyone educate him, never passed examinations, and so many nights had finished in saloons in tests of strength and masculine integrity, stepping outside with another to extend argument into the one decision, who could hit hardest. It was no use saying he did not understand it. He understood it fine, because he liked it, but knowing Gilligan had wrecked some of the joy he still took in it. He was older now, more mature, surely, mature enough to know that to be best; to be really tops, he would have to defeat everyone in the world, knock out everybody, shoot every lion, have every woman, demolish the whole population of the world. He burst out laughing and Jama watched him as he pegged strips of meat on sticks near the glowing red fire.

It was funny because it was serious, for you could be as reasonable as you liked but you had to leave this country with a Gilligan in it who could never say, "But I cut Muller down to size in the end. He couldn't really take it after all." Yes, Gilligan, tired and asleep, would still be Gilligan tomorrow, a guy watching Muller getting tired. That crack about the binoculars and his eyesight had been gnawing at him all day, and it was good that it did, because it reminded him that Gilligan had not and would never give up. The necessary stupidity of it, the inescapable truth that it mattered vitally to both of them that one of them should be accepted by the other as superior. And because he was so tired, he, Muller, knew he must follow that elephant until he got it, and Gilligan must be there to endure with him, to see the elephant got, and to say, "I'm through. I'm all in," and to think, for he would think it all right, 'You're the toughest one I've ever come across.'

"And all because you started me off wrong, all because you made it plain from the start that you thought you were the greatest guy in the world," Muller said aloud, his eyes on the stars.

"What the hell's biting you now, Muller?" Gilligan asked from across the fire in the darkness. Muller turned on his side and saw Gilligan sitting with a glowing cigarette in his hand. "Still working out your problems of how to understand a bush stiff like me? Do you think I think I'm the greatest guy in the world?" He let out a coughing laugh mixed with cigarette smoke.

"So you've come to, have you? Jeeze but you looked peaceful snoring there." Muller had quickly recovered from his confusion at his thoughts being overheard. He was going a little screwy himself, no doubt about it; this country soon got you, no kidding.

"None of this was worth Chongu," said Gilligan bitterly. "None of it."

"You want to rub it in about how you reckon if I'd shot that elephant where you think I didn't hit it, then Chongu would be alive right now? Is that it?"

"Yes, that's it. But we'll leave that one behind too. The thing is tomorrow. What time do you want to start? I'm for going now. The moon's coming up. You could read a book by it when it's right up. O.K.? Or are you more tired than I think?"

"Fine," Muller said. "We'll eat this meat and we'll pull out. The elephant must be in that forest out that way," he pointed into the darkness. "It looked about seven miles to me."

"To you it might look seven miles. But it's more like twenty as a matter of fact," Gilligan said, with not too much evident satisfaction. He felt despair with his long experience, the weight of his age.

"So I'm wrong again?" Muller was bright, bitter, and intense.

"You're right. You're wrong again." To Jama, Gilligan said, "Serve that meat up and fast too. We're moving."

They ate the hot meat in edgy and uncomfortable silence squatting by the fire. Then they picked up their rifles and Jama gathered up the utensils and put them in his haversack.

The whole world of wilderness was brightly lit now with bluish white brilliance. Far off they could hear jackals. As they began to march Muller was thinking, 'You could die here and nobody'd know. How much do I want that goddam elephant really?' He never knew how much he really wanted anything. Nobody did, which was some comfort. Gilligan was stepping it out as if he had lost ten years in age.

'This guy's going to see me beat if I don't look out,' Muller fretted. 'And I *know* he's thinking about it all the time. Remember it's not a joke. It's the real thing. Don't weaken. Don't think too many things. I'm on trial every minute. And he's old and finished, and I'm young. And all that kind of vital crap. Yes, vital.'

32

"You do understand, Muller, that I've never been up this far before," said Gilligan. "That means water. Water. Just a word. But I don't know if you've ever been without it for long."

They were crossing hilly country strewn with great lumps of blackish stone which had been flung across the country by an explosion in other times, and the light was beginning to seep into the sky in a thin, gray luminous veil. Faint dew had fallen upon them. It was cool. They dreaded the sun waiting far down below the world, his first warning already there on the sharp, black undulating skyline in a faint golden quivering. Gilligan had been right about the forest. It was much farther than Muller had thought, but Gilligan did not mention it again. He knew now there was no need to do so with a man as vain as himself, knew that Muller would always remember it as a little but important failure. Muller did not reply to Gilligan's words about water, so Gilligan spoke of it again.

"There's water all right, but you never know how far you have to go to it. There are water holes all over this country, used by the nomadic tribes, but you might have to go without it for a while. It's a matter of luck. What I'm getting at—"

"I know what you're getting at. We'll get the elephant today and that's it. If there's no water here then we know there's water behind us. We've got full canteens of water on Jama's back. I can take it, pal. You watch me."

"Listen, Muller, all I'm saying is that if you want to go after this elephant into country like this which I haven't been in before, then be prepared to go thirsty. I don't mean thirst as you may have known it. I mean *thirst*. Now for God's sake don't start anything about who can go longest. I'm just mentioning what may be a fact. We may have to go thirsty until we get back to our last camp. On the other hand we may not have to."

"O.K. Fine. But I know you now. You never say a word without some meaning in it. You never let up, I know that. You think I can't go without water. Yes, you do. I know that voice of yours now, boy, like I know a phonograph record I've played too often. Well, watch me. Watch how long I can go without water."

"All *right*," Gilligan said angrily. "I will. I'll watch. Get yourself all worked up again. All right. By God I'll see to it that I never—"

"Never take on anyone like me again, someone you can't whip, someone with a will like your own. It's O.K. with me, Gilligan. I *like* it." 'Jeezus, I'm getting as insane as Gilligan,' Muller was thinking.

"You've had a touch of the sun, Muller."

"There's Gavai," Jama shouted from behind them. "That little slave with the bow. See him there. *Huku. Huku.*" Jama pointed to Gavai who was running, like a small ant, down the side of a dry yellow hill toward the party.

"Well, what do you know," Muller said.

"Have a look with the binoculars," Gilligan murmured, smiling at Muller.

"I don't need the goddam binoculars," Muller said, a threat in his eyes.

"Don't you? Well, I do, and I've got better eyes than you have." And Gilligan stopped and studied Gavai through the binoculars while Muller, wrong again, glowered at him.

"Anything unusual?" Muller asked.

"He's running hard to reach us. If you ask me that little bastard went on and trailed those elephants. Once these hunters start on a hunt they usually can't leave off, and poor old Chongu told me that all the little bastard wants is all the tobacco I can give him. Shall we sit and wait for him?"

"You can sit if you want to."

"Ah, God, you get on my bloody wick, Muller, you get on my bloody wick." Gilligan strode ahead, leaving Muller behind.

It was ten minutes before Gavai reached them and Gilligan had guessed right. Gavai had followed the elephants. When he had finished listening to Gavai's fantastic Ki-Swahili, and Jama had been allowed to strain some of it through a Somali dialect, Gilligan told Muller that the elephants were moving slowly, and that they had the wounded bull with them. The old bull was pretty sick but was moving under his own power, though very slowly.

"How long will it take us to reach them?"

"It's taken Gavai a day to reach us here," Gilligan told him, grim and disappointed by Gavai's news. "It might take us two or three days."

"That's hooey," Muller said. "If the old bull is moving slowly and it's taken Gavai a day to reach us, then we can hurry and make them by tomorrow." He lost his temper then. "Listen, Gilligan, I'm paying you a lot of dough. Right? How about showing a little more enthusiasm? How about being a white hunter and leading me to that bull?"

"I'm not in a hurry any more, Muller. We'll get to the bull all right." Gilligan looked amused as he said this to the hard-breathing Muller. "Don't shout at me like that. You had your chance to kill the bull, and you missed. So we're walking our bloody feet off because you missed. Now cut out the evasion and let's have no more lectures, please."

They did not speak to each other for over three hours after that, and Muller did not call for his water bottle from Jama, and he was quietly amused to see that Gilligan did not call for his either. They were at it again. Fine. Anything he could do, the other could better. O.K. Let it be.

33

THE LONG, SWEATING, THIRSTING DAY pinched a flame out in Muller. Until today he had always drunk more water than Gilligan, who was used to a much smaller amount of it than he was, and by the time dusk came Muller was almost out on his feet, with his tongue swollen in his hot, dry mouth. He almost wrenched the water bottle out of Jama's hands when he saw Gilligan breaking his own fast, and Gilligan laughed at him as he greedily sucked the water down his throat.

"So nobody won that round," Gilligan said. "Want to try it again tomorrow?" He could not understand his distorted affection for Muller.

"I wonder why you get on my goddam nerves so much, Gilligan." Muller's face was shining with the spilled water. He looked as if he could murder his companion.

"We'll never solve that one." Gilligan sat down very

slowly on a cooling rock. He was almost ready to fall on his face but he had clenched everything together in him for this last stage of their safari. He was going to win, no matter what happened.

They slept out that night after eating the remains of the buck which Jama had wrapped in a wet cloth.

At midday the next day they came upon the fresh dung of the elephants. Gavai said they were not more than a couple of miles ahead. Immediately the two white men were refreshed by this news, their hunters' lust awakened again. In the privacy of his skull Gilligan had decided to shoot the old bull himself, and as a gesture of the anger he felt for the elephants, to shoot the young bull which had caused that mad stampede. He feared that young bull now more than the old one which had killed Pratt.

"There they are," he said, pointing to the herd of elephants which were in a hollow about half a mile away.

Not even Jama's marvelous eyesight saw the old bull and his companion standing in thick gray bush about a hundreds yards away on their right front, and Gilligan, despite his quickened hunter's appetite, was too weary to be as cautious as usual.

"Come on, then," he said, knowing that he must finish all his long fantasy here at last, for he was going to pick out the old and the young bulls and murder them both in the coldest possible blood. He had had enough of himself and of Muller, and of this safari, and he was miserable physically, longing to lie down. Live or die now, he wanted an end to a mystery.

The three of them were not ready at all for what

happened next; though their rifles were ready, their mental and physical mechanisms were not.

The old bull, too sick to move any further for a while, was standing in that peculiar elephant stillness under a thorn tree, a patchwork of bluish shadow and golden glare on his back, when he smelled the men who did not suspect his nearness. He lifted his head and pressed back his ears and the young bull, alarmed, came fast out of the trees and smelled the men as well, and went straight for Gilligan who was in front. The old bull wheeled slowly and made off and Muller saw him first and went running after him, leaving Gilligan bringing up his rifle in shocked amazement as the young bull, not fifty yards away now, came at him in what looked like a venomous and relentless charge out of ambush. His head was high. It would have to be a chest shot. Too late, he knew his heart was not in it. He did not want to shoot anything any more. But he had to.

Gilligan's bullet smashed into the bull's chest, tearing through him like a small blazing comet, and while it shook him it was not big enough to overcome his rage and his demented strength. There was no time to get the second barrel in, for Gilligan went flying into the air, turning over and over from the violent lifting blow the dying beast had delivered him. His rifle was sailing in the other direction, passing over Jama's head. The elephant, dead now on his feet, went into a sprawling, driving crash along the ground not far from Jama, spraying blood from his trunk all over the crouching Somali, who grinned with fear and excitement.

Gilligan came hurtling down on his back among rocks and fallen trees, a terrible scream forced from him by the shock of his fall, and then he uttered one dry, gurgling cry of agony, for he was broken. The pain obliterated everything, rubbed out his mind and left nothing in his head but a series of desperate, silent cries. He was coming out of unconsciousness when Jama found him.

"Don't touch me," he screamed as Jama reached out his hands to lift him, and then, sweat pouring from his face, he swallowed again and again, his eyes closed. "Don't touch me," he said in a low voice. He was all broken and he knew he was finished. He wanted to lie there and not be touched, and his flesh knew best, and it was thinking for him, as if he had seen into his own broken back and all his fractured bones. He kept fainting and coming to while Jama leaned over him and watched him with un-blinking eyes, tense, tender, fearful.

"The elephant is dead," Jama said. "See his blood." He grinned and exhibited himself, holding out his arms, and through his narrowed, screwed-up eyes Gilligan saw all the blood. Jama was soaked with it, dripping with it, and he shook with laughter when Gilligan smiled thinly with down-turned lips.

"Get the whisky out of my pocket," Gilligan whispered, and then his voice strengthened. "But don't push me or move me. Here, in this pocket, there's a flask." Tenderly Jama drew the big leather-covered flask from Gilligan's pocket, inch by inch, his eyes fixed on Gilligan's face until he had it free from the pocket.

"Pour some into my mouth," said Gilligan, and then, frantic again, "but don't pour it too fast. Slowly. Slowly." There was threat and terror in his eyes as he looked at Jama. He wanted to be treated with care and tenderness. He did not want any stupid bungling or he would faint, again, but he fainted before Jama got the flask to his lips.

"*Tembu ndege mbaya kwangu,*" he said wearily when the slow drips of whisky into his throat awakened him. "I should have left the elephants alone. I knew it. I knew it." He saw Jama again and said, "Tell Aganaza to make tea and to get the truck ready." The pain seized him through his daze then and took him in its teeth like a lion and crunched him, Jama gripping his wrist as Gilligan's cries strangled in his working throat.

"You are finished, Bwana," Jama said. "What do you want me to do? It is a long way to Aganaza at the camp."

"Camp?"

"The camp."

"Cigarette. Pocket. Careful now." He shouted it again, "Careful now." Jama took some minutes to get the cigarettes out of the right-hand pocket of Gilligan's bush shirt. He put one in Gilligan's mouth and lit it for him. It took a few minutes to achieve. Then Jama sat on his heels and watched him, plucking the cigarette from Gilligan's mouth and putting it back again at sensible intervals, and Gilligan dreamed and sweated, trying to tie down his mind again in his blazing head.

"Whisky." Jama obeyed and dripped whisky slowly into Gilligan's open mouth, his lips moving in silence. Allah the Beneficent, the Merciful. There is no God but death, and living is his prophet.

"Enough. *Basi. Natosha,*" Gilligan sighed and opened his eyes and looked at the sky. "Where's the other Bwana?" he asked. "Dead? Dead?" Jama shook his head, grinning.

"He's gone after the old elephant," he said. "I will go

and see what I can see. There is a hill not far from here."
'We come, and we go. And we are lucky to have been.'

"Don't be long. Hurry back." Gilligan heard Jama
running across the sand. "Come back. Come back," he
cried frantically, and then silenced himself, growling and
cursing, his eyes closing.

"You're finished, Bwana." Gilligan said it aloud. "You're
finished, Bwana. I'm Bwana now, don't have to shout for
it. That's it, though, the fact. The fact. Africa speaks.
You're finished, Bwana." A sharper, colder-minded Africa,
though, Somali, of a race for whom death was less, much
less than it was for the softer, chunkier, darker Africa of
Aganaza and so many others. "You're dying," the Somali
said. Yes. When you were old and done for, as a Somali
behind the camels, nothing was said on that last morning
when the others watched you stagger in your age to your
feet, and nothing was said when you fell down in the
burning sand behind the camels. Nobody looked back.
You were old, gone, left behind. Same thing, though, in
another way farther south in Aganaza's Africa where you
were hurled when dead, to the hyenas, who dragged you
up and down for days. Finished, Bwana. And fair enough
too. We come. We go. We leave a diminishing stain.
Then we vanish, forgotten.

"Fair enough," he cried as the pain swamped him again.
Soon he heard Jama coming back, padding across the
sand, his shadow falling on Gilligan's eyes.

"The Bwana has gone a long way. I can see nothing of
him," said Jama. "That old elephant does not want to be
killed. You want a cigarette, whisky?"

"Whisky, and then a cigarette."

A delirium started halfway through the cigarette which Jama held over his mouth.

"*Sababu?*" he began in Ki-Swahili. "Why? Knew all the time it was fatal. Leave well alone. Leave something undone, that's the thing and I knew that all right, take my tip. *Wewe na jua sana*, Jama. *Mimi na jua. Huyu na jua. Sisi na jua. Mungu na jua. Na tembu na jua.* He knew, you, I, we, they, we all knew. All knew and the elephants knew. Come on, then. We're here. Waiting. Follow us. Come in. Catch us, if you can. Impossible, I tell you. *Wapi* Bwana Muller?"

"Bwana Muller *na tembia, na tafuta tembu*," Jama said patiently. "He is hunting the elephant, far off."

"All right for him. Wonder what *his* worry is? Mine's elephant. His too I'll bet. Or no? I knew, though, I knew it all the time. Money. I took his money. Want his money. Would never have come back here except for his money. Wilderness, chum. You go on and on, no end, and it's all theirs, this country. Plenty of nothing all around. Money, though, that's the thing. I'm paying top prices for this so come on, jack yourself up and face everything. You're sick." He stared at Jama. "Jama," he said. "I'm sick."

"Very sick," Jama said, nodding.

"Finished. That's what you said. *Nekwisha.* Finished. Yes. Said O.K. I'll do it, for the money. *Wapi* Bwana Muller?"

"He's gone after the old elephant."

Gilligan stared at Jama for a long time without speaking, moaning faintly in his throat, and the delirium faded from his eyes and he spoke hoarsely.

"You're all bloody," he said. "I did that. The elephant

is dead. Wrong elephant. But dead. He waited for me, that young one. He was waiting. I knew I should not come on this safari, Jama. I knew it."

"It is your luck," Jama told him. "You were meant to die here. Now you die. That is all there is, luck." He smiled in a friendly way at Gilligan. He was a truly religious man.

"That's because you're a Somali you say that," Gilligan said. "But it's not like that at all. It only looks like it. I could say I knew I would get bad luck up here with the elephants. They're all right, elephants. No harm in them. No, it's not luck. It's just stupid, that's all." He shouted it, despite the pain it brought on. "Stupid."

Jama poured some more whisky down Gilligan's throat. "Get drunk, Bwana," he said. "Is it hurting now?"

"It's hurting all right." Gavai appeared then, panting, the little, squat, black, shining man standing over Gilligan and getting his breath.

"The other Bwana sent me back to call you," he said. "He is going on after the elephant. The elephants do not stop. Again they came back and took the old bull but the Bwana is going on after them. He will never reach them. They are hurrying away." He stared at Jama upon whom the blood was drying now.

"This white man is dying," Jama said solemnly. "The elephant struck him. He is dying. How will you get your tobacco now?" He smiled at Gavai's worried eyes. "Go, run all the way, and tell Aganaza to come, and tell him to send back for the truck."

"I don't want to hear about the elephants," Gilligan said wearily. "Don't talk to me about elephants, but get the Bwana Muller. Bring him back. He's wasting his time. He's going too far. He is mad. Go and bring him here."

"What am I to do?" Gavai said to Jama, his eyes haunted by all this worry and by the threat about the tobacco in Jama's eyes.

34

FOR THE SECOND TIME Muller came on his own tracks, and this time he was afraid. He had slept out alone the night before, cursing Gilligan who was sitting on his ass back there contented now that he had at last shot an elephant.

Muller had looked back the afternoon before and had seen the young bull lying dead, and shifting his binoculars he had seen Jama moving about. So Gilligan had shot an elephant at last.

"Come on, you decrepit bastard," he had yelled from nearly a mile away, "you've shot your elephant. O.K. Now come on and earn some more bucks." He had turned away after that and had trotted on after the old bull. He saw it rejoin the herd just before dusk, and he had sat down and smoked a cigarette and tried to decide what to do. He had to have that bull no matter what.

With the lump of metal in its head, half crazy with

pain, the old bull swung onward with the herd which had closed around him. Gavai had watched them rescue him and had stayed where he was until they had gone. When he went back to Muller there was a long and bewildering time in which the white man had talked, shouted, and then screamed in his own language, all the while pointing with his finger back to where the other Bwana must be. And Gavai, guessing at last, though fearful, had run all the miles back to find Gilligan lying on his back with Jama beside him.

Muller was up before dawn, thirsty, staring out at the rolling wastes of sand and thorn trees, at the high rocks which he knew would be quivering and shaking with heat in a few hours. There was still no sign of Gilligan. He raged and shouted aloud as he walked up and down beside the place he had slept the night. And he went on after the old bull. He had wounded it, "missed it" as Gilligan loved to say, and if he went to the end of the earth after the bastard he would get it. Had to have it. Must. If he went all out he could get it. He had no doubt of it. Just use the will, that's all. And he was on his own now. No more bitching and fighting with that maniac, Gilligan. On. On.

He lost the trail of the herd not long after sunrise, but he went on, confident that his instincts would guide him. It was a long time before he admitted that he was lost, and when he came on his own tracks for the second time, and the first astounding fear fell upon him, he looked around him at the wilderness as if seeing it for the first time. It seemed to announce that he did not matter in any way, that it was here for all time, and that he was not. He stood looking around it with frightened eyes for a long time, the sun overhead like an inferno which had silenced the whole world. There were no birds, no beasts, no sounds of anything living. In the far distances were faint blue mountains, and beyond, he knew, was more and more wilderness, and he shrank. No man would ever be the king of the world.

"Now take it easy, kid," he said. "Relax. Start all over again and find your tracks. *Don't* panic." But he went running, his head bent, his eyes searching the dust and the sand for his own sign, and he kept finding it, all of it, all of the sign he had been making in his desperate searches all day. His tongue was stuck to the roof of his mouth.

The next morning he woke up as the sun hit his eyelids with scalding light. He tore off his shirt and began to suck the thin dew from it, frantic, and saying, "Take it easy, kid, you're in trouble."

The red dawn came up in wave after wave of bloody light, and he watched it in wonder and fear as it spread over the sky, the elephants forgotten. He had to get out of here. There was no end to this country he had run into. Go back. He started to walk in the direction he felt certain must be back, but his head was not his own any more. It was swirling with streams of curses and accusations, against himself, Gilligan, and against the elephants, until it all mingled in one stream of frightened chatter.

35

"HAVE YOU PACKED THE AMMUNITION?" Gilligan said. "There should be ten cases of Bren gun magazines."

"Yes, Bwana," said Jama. Gilligan was weaker now. Jama poured the last drops of whisky into his trembling lips.

"Water drums full?"

"All full, Bwana." Again and again Gilligan had raved.

"Right. Tell the convoy commander to start. Vehicles to be two hundred yards apart until we pass the water point. Tell the sergeant major that convoy discipline is his responsibility. I'll break the bastard if it's like yesterday. Got that?"

"Yes, Bwana."

"Cigarette. Come on, pull finger. Cigarette. *Futa* bloody *kidole yaku.* Cigarette." Jama lit the last cigarette for him.

"Now I'll tell you the facts, Muller, and I want no bloody back chat until I've finished. See? Don't start

248

blinding me with science because I can't stand it. You can keep the money. I want it, don't fool yourself, I want it, but I'm not taking it. This was your idea. This trip. My God, when I think of the things I've put up with for your money I could shoot myself. Forget it, chum. This time *I'm* speaking. As for Graig and the money you gave him I'll send it to you. Money's nothing, chum, until you get windy. All right, I was windy. I wanted that money. Old? Me, old? Well, yes, old. O.K. Needed the money. Well, you can keep it, chum. Ram it. I don't need it. I've done my piece. Here are the facts. Elephants hate money. Did you know about that? Write a check and give it to that old bull and you'll see. They don't want it. You twisted my bloody arm but I walked you flat. I love elephants. I do, you know. Forget all that stuff I told you. I trusted you and you said I was sick. O.K. Well, never again, chum. Where's Jama?"

"I'm here, Bwana."

"Now I'm going to tell you again, Jama. You call Bwana Muller here and tell him to face me. He got me up here, for money. You tell him to come here and face me. Go on."

"Bwana Muller is hunting the elephant," Jama said once again. "He will come back tomorrow."

"They should be left alone, all the elephants. All of them. God damn it, there are only one or two things I want to say to him." He closed his eyes and fell into silence. Jama got up and began to make tea. It would be two days before Gavai, even traveling as fast as a hunter, could reach Aganaza, and the white man would be dead by then.

"Jama. Jama."

"Bwana."

"Come here."

"What is it, Bwana?"

"You always call me Bwana now without being told to. Why is that?"

"I don't know, Bwana."

"What are you going to do?"

"You mean about work?"

"I don't know what I mean. How do I know what I mean?"

"I'm going to America with Bwana Muller. I asked him to take me."

Gilligan began to laugh, moaning in the middle of his laughter as the pain broke on top of him again.

"You've no need to go to America now, Jama," he said. "America is coming to you. It's here. Here. Everywhere. No need to go to America. You're finished, Bwana. You said that to me, didn't you. Didn't you."

"You want tea, Bwana?"

"I want nothing any more. I'm tired out. Whisky."

"The whisky is finished."

"Typical. Typical."

"Why you hate Somali mans?" Jama said sharply, bending over Gilligan to look into his wild hot blue eyes.

"You're too bloody independent, that's why," Gilligan replied in English, gripping Jama's wrist. "You're not innocent. You're not soft. You're not a patch on Aganaza. He was trustful."

"Tomorrow I will go and find Bwana Muller," Jama said slowly, almost into Gilligan's ear. "He is a good man."

"I wasted my bloody life," said Gilligan. "That's what

I did. Don't tell me about elephants or any nonsense like that. I was good for years until you came along. But you can have it all, Muller, I had the best of it, though, saw it when it was new and all fine and not messed up. The park keepers are feeding the lions on slices of cold zebra in the game reserves and the Masai have to look on. The lions know they're safe and the Masai know they can't kill the lions, and the will has gone on both sides. I've seen it, I tell you. You can have it, all of it. You mean to tell me that's any use to me, that kind of thing? I tell you for the last time you can have it." A feeling of wilderness.

It was dark when he began to die. Jama had lit a huge fire not far from where Gilligan lay. He sat beside Gilligan and watched him die. 'We are born, and then we die. *Wallahi!*'

"Tea, Bwana," he said, holding a tin mug of cool tea to Gilligan's lips. Gilligan shook his head and then cried sharply aloud with a beginning of final pain. "*Bado Kidogo.*"

"All men to report with gym kit at sixteen hundred hours," he said to the sky. "Now, unarmed combat. Rush me. Come on. Don't play about. This isn't a game. Rush me. Right. Down on one knee like so, shoulder into the opponent's stomach, then lift and swing. You're down. Next man! Dismiss! The prodigal son. Now there was a young corporal went into a far country and spent his substance, squandered his pay, and would fain fill his belly with the husks that the swine did eat. And one day he arose and said I will go to my father and say father I have come unto you your son that was lost. And he went to his father and his father who had just been made up to sergeant, fell upon his neck and kissed him, and then, looking into the corporal's eyes, he shouted, ONE PACE STEP BACK, MARCH!" Gilligan was trying to get up, laughing crazily, shouting, "You see, you bloody rookies, you don't know your drill. One pace step back, march!" Jama held him and lowered him onto his back again. Gilligan uttered a long, tremulous sigh and died.

36

MULLER SEIZED THE WATER BOTTLE that Jama held out
to him, gripped it like a starving baby, and clamped his
mouth onto it and drank, sobbing with gratitude and
madness. Jama smiled and held onto the bottle until he
thought Muller had had enough. Then he tore it away
from him, fighting to get it back.

"Is long way back to camp," he said. "You have more
waters, soon." Muller fell back under the rock where
Jama had found him and lay on his face. Jama poured
water over his hair and neck, saying, "You go too far for
elephant. Elephant gone home." He had to give Muller
more water or fight him, for Muller dragged himself out
of the shade and tried to get Jama by the throat, Jama
fighting him off gently and laughing, though quietly angry
as well. He wrenched the water bottle away again from
Muller's lips and walked up and down for a time while
Muller tried to focus his eyes on him. It was some hours

until Muller realized he was safe, was found, was going to live. He took hold of Jama's hands and stared up into his eyes.

"You're a great guy," he kept saying. "A great guy." He fell asleep after that and Jama made a fire and started a kettle boiling for tea. He had shot a lone oryx bull with the .318 some miles back and he had brought the liver and some of the meat with him in his haversack. He sang a song about a raid made by a Dolbohanta clan on the Abyssinians of the Ogaden in the old days, one eye on Muller who was asleep on his face.

He had the tea and the meat ready when he woke Muller nearly an hour later. Muller looked at him hard, resting on his elbows, and then he looked out at the oceans of scrub and rock-strewn sand.

"It's a big country, too big, too big," he said, as if speaking to himself. He looked at Jama.

"Bwana Gilligan's dead, isn't he?" he said. Jama nodded.

"Elephant kill him," he said. "After he kill elephant he die."

"I knew it. He would have come, wouldn't he." Muller put his face in his hands and lowered his head. "Dead," he said.

It was such a strange grief he felt then that for some moments he thought it was for Gilligan, and in a way it was, but it was for all men who never got quite what they sought all their lives, only something resembling it, the wrong and unexpected elephant. The unattainable was the thing to go for, the thing no one else could get, and which no one was ever going to get, not even he, Muller. As this dark spirit of sorrow invaded him, the premonition of age and death, the enemy Gilligan had practiced with every day of his life, fear of one day not being alive at all, he had one of those swift moments of vision when he thought he saw and knew everything, and he looked up at the sky, and the vision was gone, fled, like a bird which had passed through his skull. The dolor of the meaning of death, which had had him so nearly solved in its hands, until Jama came with the holy water into his madness, seeped into his will while he thought of how he had been the machinery which had dragged Gilligan to his final appointment.

'Fine. Fine. You're doing fine. Get really sad, but what the hell, you've been sweated down, tired, scared, and dying of thirst, terrified, and now it's all O.K. A hand appears with a water bottle, you drink, and death gets washed away, so it's all O.K. Tomorrow you'll want to kick a rhino's ass again, for pleasure.' That was true. He was laughing quietly and Jama, roasting meat over the fire, was watching him.

'That's what you get like when you've been really frightened, like a feeling you're ready for the armchair and the slippers and no more adventure of any kind. But you hand me that meat when it's ready, Jama, and when I've pushed it down into the incinerator we'll open a fresh box, I'll spit in a snake's eye. You see.'

The big bull appeared in his skull, came over the horizon of his mind, and he knew he was well again, ready to live and to do and to go on, right down the line again. Impatience came and swept away the melancholy invader, the whisperer who said, "Why are you doing all this? What's the point?" On. On.

Jama handed him hot meat on a stick. Muller devoured it all in a few seconds and Jama gave him another stick with pieces of roasted liver on it and he ate that just as fast. He ate everything Jama gave him, totally absorbed in his appetite. When the meat was finished he got to his feet and leaned against the rock.

"I've got ten rounds of .500 ammunition on me, Jama," he said. "We'll look around for tracks and follow those elephants. That bull must have had to stop again. Pack the kit and we'll move. I'm O.K. now. We'll take it nice and slow for the first couple of hours."

Jama laughed and pointed to the sun.

"Is late now, Bwana," he said. "Is too late catch elephant." The boyish eagerness of Muller was not like that of most white men he had known. It was different, was likable and too young. It did not know its real strength, which was death, as well as life. Muller did not understand death. Not like Gilligan.

"Come on, get up and let's get moving."

"No, Bwana. You not catch elephant. They go on and on until we lost and die." Jama was grave now, shaking his head and stirring the fire with a long branch. "You not know this country, Bwana." Muller began to shout at him and Jama watched him and listened, unmoved. When Muller had finished shouting he said, "Jama not go with you. You die up there if you go. You die here if Jama not come with water."

"I've got to have the goddam bull," Muller shouted. "Don't you tell me what to do, Jama, I've got to kill that bull. It means everything to me. Now get up and come on. You're on the pay roll now. Let's get moving."

"Chongu dead. Bwana dead. All will die, Bwana. You not go." Jama looked sternly at him and stood up. "No shout at Jama. You not like Bwana Gilligan. He old-time mans, strong and hard mans, hunter mans. Is dead. He know elephant. You rich mans. Why you want die here like this? Why you not live in house and eat food and drink? Why you do this?"

"You don't understand," Muller cried. "It's important. I thought you were brave. I thought you were tough. Now are you coming or not?" He knew he could not go if Jama would not go with him. "I'll give you all the money you want," he said. "Is it money you want?"

"I work for you but I not go for elephant. You not catch that elephant. Jama know."

Muller sat down in the shade again and looked accusingly into Jama's hard eyes.

"So you won't go?" he said.

"That elephant make you follow till you die. He take you far till you finish. He kill everybody. Jama not go."

"Then I've got to go myself. It's a challenge and I can't back down now." He forgot Jama and spoke urgently to the rocks, to the plains, to himself. "Gilligan was a great guy. I hated his guts but he was a great guy. He didn't have what it takes but I respect him for that. He knew he had it coming to him, and he went and he took it. O.K. Open a fresh box. But it's big now, this thing, it's got to be finished." He looked at Jama with accusing eyes, going on to say, "I rescued you, you bastard, when you were on your ass in the bush—*he* did that to you and I saved your life, and now you've saved mine, so we're quits. O.K. Then open a fresh box. What are you laughing at, you bastard, eh? Would you laugh at Bwana Gilligan? Would you?" Jama was holding one hand over his mouth as if pretending to hide his laughter.

"You not save Jama," he said, trying to stop laughing.

"Jama Somali mans, go days no water, no food, bush nothing for Somali mans. Bwana Gilligan he know that. He want insult me not kill me. He not kill Jama that way. You not know *dasturi*, Bwana, you not know tings of custom." He stopped laughing and stood up. "You want go for die. Jama not come. Is big country, plenty heat, elephants go on. They not let you kill that old one, he their God, like their God same as God." He shook his head. "Two mens die now. Jama not go now. You come back now, Bwana, all finish with old elephant. You lost. I find you here wit nottings, like old woman you die here if Jama not come."

"Listen to me." Muller took Jama's arm, and Jama slowly withdrew it from Muller's hand, another *dasturi* that Muller did not know—you do not take Somalis by the arm this way. "O.K. Take your goddam arm back, then, but listen to me. You don't understand, Jama. I'm committed. You know, *committed*, signed on, like it was a *promise*, I'm committed, I've promised that bull to a museum in my home town. I'm from the big family there, you see, I mean the dough and the leading this and that and the leading family and everything. Skip it. Don't frown. Just listen. O.K. They didn't come in the *Mayflower*—that was the biggest goddam ship ever built, I know, but the Muller's weren't on it. It was all later, but we're solid, and we've got dough and position, and when a Muller says he's giving the biggest elephant ever built to the museum, well that's it, you see. And it means something more than just the museum—"

"What is museum?" Jama asked him. "Is factory?"

"Museum," Muller said thoughtfully, tiredly, staring at Jama's steady eyes and reminded of the human museum of Africa in which he stood. "Skip it," he went on. "I've promised to kill that elephant. It's wounded, it's all shot and it'll fall down somewhere in the end, and it's the biggest there is left in the world. Anyone will tell you that. You ever seen a bigger elephant than that one? Have you?"

"Is big," Jama said. "Is bigger elephants in my country, plenty bigger elephants. Is nothing, that bull, to what I see in my country—"

"You're a goddam liar, Jama." Muller leaned forward until he was close to Jama. "You're not talking to some kid or tourist now, Jama. So cut the crap will you, and listen to me. I'm asking you for the last time, will you come on with me until I've shot that elephant?" Jama shook his head and refused again.

"You're frightened," said Muller. "You're scared out of your pants. O.K. But just admit that, will you? You're afraid it'll kill you. Right?"

Jama looked at him proudly, sneering with anger, straightening his back before he replied.

"Somali mans cannot be afraid," he said, husky with rage when he thought of being called afraid, and then he smiled, looking cunning and playful. "You not make Jama go wit saying afraid. Come, Bwana. Leave elephants their country. Come back. You Bwana now, Gilligan dead. Men want Bwana here, go back to Janali Ganjo River to truck. Jama not care, but slave peoples, Aganaza and other mens waiting for Bwana. Is your work, to be helping mens, paying mens, safari finished."

Despair showed in Muller's face. He could not go it alone and he knew it, and he knew that the elephants would draw him on into red dawn after red dawn, and you did not have to be lost to be lost. He was lost now. He did not know where he was. Jama knew, even though Jama had not been here before. He was beaten, and anyway, the elephants did not know he was beaten. They only wanted to live their life, their useless life, away from the gunmen and the out-of-date collectors of heads and skins, and hunting was out of date, even though he loved it. And it was not the same with Gilligan dead. Maybe he could get another white hunter, one less screwy than Gilligan, a hunter who would do what he was told and who would not give exhibitions of strength, would not want to show how great he was; a hunter who was not old but who had new ideas and could work in on a problem and have fun as well. No. Gilligan had been O.K., except for that feeling he had had that he was better than Muller, who had all the dough in the world, and who resented Muller for being good, and for being the employer. All for a goddam elephant.

"Elephant he die anyway, even if you not kill him, Bwana," Jama said. "You leave him, he die. You follow he get angry, kill you, have to kill you. You make elephants strong. Come, we go back."

Tiny on the wilderness, the two men retreated, Jama leading, Muller lost in desperate thoughts, yet he wanted to live, make new plans, think, for he would die if he went further and he knew it. And in a strange way, he felt glad too, and that was worse.

He thought of outwalking Jama on the way back, of really showing Jama where to get off physically and morally, but Jama was not white, and there was not the same kick in wanting to beat Jama, and this was Jama's country and anyway he was tough all right. No, forget it.

He felt older, and now that there was no Gilligan to march beside in unspoken antagonism he began to explore himself, to become bored and listless, and Jama led him and kept the pace.

Once Muller turned around and looked at the world belonging to the elephants. It stretched everywhere, and it looked terrifying now, to think that he had been going to lose himself in it, drawn on and on after an obsolete shape, when there was really no need, for after all—

He could not finish that thought, but he spoke to the wilderness, saying, "Well, you didn't get me after all; maybe. And then again you may have got me, because I'll want to come back." He heard Jama laughing. He turned round and saw Jama looking at him, smiling.

"Go on, laugh," Muller said, not really annoyed. "But it gets you, this country. You lose your goddam head in it. I *might* have made it. I might have got that bull if I went on, and now I'll never know."

"Is plenty elephants, Bwana. Plenty everywhere wit not hard country like that one up there where you die for water."

"Yeah, but where's the challenge? Eh?" He saw Jama's puzzled look again. "Challenge," he said again. "You don't know what challenge is?" Jama shook his head.

"It's something that drives you crazy, Jama," was all he could think to say.

"No water in sun. That drive you crazy."

"Yeah?" Muller smiled thinly. "Well, lead on, and show me the way back to an eventual T-bone steak and my automobile's twice as long as yours."

An uneasy peace settled on Muller as he followed Jama again. He felt he had not proved himself, had been talked into retreat by a black man with no conception of the bitterness he, Muller, felt. And then again, Jama might know. Might.

ABOUT THE AUTHOR

GERALD HANLEY spent over seven years in the more wild and isolated areas of East Africa, four and a half of them wandering in Somalia. Before the war he farmed in Kenya. He served in the Burma campaign with an East African Division made up of many tribes. He was born in 1916 in England, of a Dublin father and a Cork mother, is an Irish citizen, and lives in County Cork.

This book was set in

Janson and Baskerville types,

printed, and bound by

The Haddon Craftsmen.

Design is by Larry Kamp.